I0713016

www.eibonvalepress.co.uk

Moonshine Express

Poppet

Moonshine Express
Poppet

Copyright 2013.

Published 01 November 2013 by Eibonvale Press
www.eibonvalepress.co.uk

Cover art by David Rix

ISBN
978-1-908125-28-6

Part 1

Black Thunder

Chapter 1

Dried blood. Seriously, the royal paint saturating each carriage is lacquered devil's blood. Some would call it burgundy, but not me. Nope. That there looks exactly like sun tarnished sacrifice prettily adorned with a neat rectangle pinstripe of fool's gold.

Sloshing through another puddle, I'm resenting this idea. Dress up posh for a free train trip only to get my patent heels saturated in smelly water thanks to the cathartic sky in a perpetual state of purge. It's another glorious grey day in Edinburgh and the Drum Major looks like a right ponce standing with bagpipes stuffed under his arm in a deluge and gale, just to welcome the philistines into his creepy cargo.

I envision much wailing and gnashing of teeth happening nearby. Not everyone adores the pipes, especially as they *also* look like they were fashioned out of dragon bones and a pouch of plundered treasure suspiciously resembling the collection purse from church.

We're little minions shuffling through gloom to board the soul train, to revisit our inequity and deliberate over our failures as productive adults in a world drenched in opportunity and entrepreneurs. What's our excuse?

Well it could be that Eden left, or it could be because mum was an alky who vanished when I was too young to remember her, or it could just be I'm a lazy cow who hates the gym and honestly praises pixies for support tights.

What was I thinking? I'm going to be the pauper here and they're all going to know it.

I checked this baby out online and noted it usually leaves from Waverley station, so why for the love of sunshine are we sent to the backwaters 'secret' departure point? We could be under cover instead of forced to wrestle with the elements like outcasts using the servants entrance.

It's all very clandestine and suspect.

Black window frames bite into panes so shiny they're portals to Perdition, shadowing my walk, mocking my bedraggled attempt at elegance. Distorted to squat and dumpling-looking, my reflection undulates in silent parody. Looking away I glare back at the piper, grateful to see a man in a long onyx trench-coat step up to him. Now I won't feel pinned to the bug board in condescending disdain when I reach them. Instead I get to share the judgement with Mister Black.

Rifling in my coat pocket I find the wrinkled card adorned with opulent swirls inviting me to this bad idea. Unearthing it, I expose it to the splats of water raining pollution into the crisp weave of luxurious card, embossed with a royal watermark.

Reaching them, I wave it vaguely at him, just wanting to get on board without becoming a spectacle. Heat itches my neck and I'm glad I'm wearing the silk scarf, it'll hide the embarrassment staining me as surely as guilt stains a soul.

"Nice noose," winks Mr Black.

Frowning at the stranger who gets a June pseudonym based purely on the apparel adorning his frame, I scowl in question. "Beg your pardon?"

"No pardon required, just commenting on your scarf. Looks like a noose waiting to throttle the life out of you. Surely you can't be comfortable with anything wrapped that securely around your neck?"

Staring up at the tit with an attitude, I say with my evil tart smile, "I miss my leash when he lets me out of the bedroom."

"Aaah..." He looks away over my head, arching scandalised eyebrows at bonnie Danny Boy in his red kilt.

"Right, can we get out of this weather then?" I ask them, wondering why we're chatting on the platform instead of embarking to avoid the seeping cold turning new paint green-black with mould. Eventually everything in this city bruises up with fetid rot, sporting shiners of mildew like the crowd down the pub after a decent Friday night.

This fair land isn't fair. Ain't nothing fair about it. Toughen up or sod off, that's how it goes.

The Pied Piper, he led everyone to their deaths didn't he? Once you fall under his spell no one will ever see you again. Why the hell do they have a piper wailing the bagpipes for us to board the train? Surely that's like black magic? It's a total voodoo curse on this trip before it's even begun.

Are we supposed to tip the Piper? I can offer him a tip off the platform but not much else. Perusing the set-up I glance around, both curious and cautious.

The short strip of red carpet is cordoned off with velvet rope the way you see at the cinema; a gentleman's crime scene preserving the scarlet fabric leading to the inner sanctum. *Blood bath this way.*

Glancing at Danny Boy again, I wonder if he feels stupid or proud dressing like that for work every day?

Mr Black gets the go ahead, and as we have identical invitations he pompously clasps my elbow and starts steering me on board behind the glitzy twined barrier rope that looks like it was made to hold back curtains of titanium. Possibly even to secure the stowaways to the back of the train until their demise is nothing more than track-bashed bones and unrecognisable thanks to the speed of the lynching locomotive.

Forced to walk the squelching red carpet which bleeds sponged rain into my shoe, the icy rush of fluid between my toes grosses me out.

Staring at my feet with every step, I watch as coagulated haemoglobin waves up my dainty court shoes to lick frigid suicide juice into the shoe-well.

Keeping the prissy charade I attempt to hold onto dignity when my foot starts squeaking across the silver sheen lining the inside of my sole, only to have to endure more humiliation at the pitying stare by the coiffure perfect damsel waiting in her precocious black power-dressing uniform, holding out an expectant hand like a fortune teller insisting we cross her palm with silver.

Danny Boy starts the patriotic dirge again when she orders, "Invitations please."

See, right there, this is what screams loser. We just made total arses of ourselves by thinking Danny Boy was the dude to show our passes to.

Withering under her penetrating stare I unclench my clammy hand and give her the rumpled card, looking as if I used it to blot my running eyeliner and then to wipe my nose.

Lord above this day is sinking into the bowels of hell now.

"Miss Dubois, Mr Dubois, welcome aboard."

Glancing at Mr Black I wonder why the heck he has my surname? French isn't that common in these parts. What are the odds of that? Almost as good as the odds I had yesterday when I was nearly mown over by the woman and her trolley trying to break the land speed record while doing a monthly stint around Tesco's.

Suddenly unsure, halfway down the nine carriage train on our way to our designated suites, I pause to ask Mr Black, "This *is* The Royal Scotsman, right?"

"I believe so, yes," he nods. "...Know a fair bit about her and if this isn't her then it's a magnificent and very costly reproduction of it."

Something doesn't feel right. The wee niggly feeling that dances the Highland Fling in my gut when something's 'off' is beyond the Fling now and gone right into a Flatley style river dance.

The problem is all I can hear is incongruous to the jig gnawing up my sixth sense, because it's a piper sounding like he's executing an infidel on the platform outside while the train bellows the screams of a dying man when it unleashes the departing whistle.

Cold trickles down my nape, forcing a formidable shudder of someone walking over my grave.

It's just rain, June. Nothing macabre, just cold water dripping out of your hair.

But your scarf prevents that.

Oh crivens! It's too late, we're moving, and Mr Black is getting impatient while I fanny about like I forgot my meds and am spaced out in a fantasy world.

It's your imagination June, get on with it girl.

Right, yes, okay, now which one of these rooms is mine?

Mr Black points at the shiny door, "That's yours I believe. Molly seems nice, doesn't she?"

"Who's Molly?" I ask, my hand already on the door handle to my suite.

"The lady who took our invites and told us to assemble in the lounge in half an hour."

"When did she say that?"

He gives me the 'you're queer' stare, "When she examined our boarding passes."

"Oh, right, yeah," I fake, giving the daft laugh and storming into my room to hide, every squeak in my shoe sounding like rusty chains abrading corrosion together.

Struck dumb, I look at the post-box accommodation with awe. Wow!

The whistle blows again as if in triumphant victory, blasting foreboding down my spine to spasm the skin sheathing my back. Dropping my bag I rub my arms briskly to stave off the sensation, tempted to block my ears at the suffering agony instilled in that whistle. It's screaming like a man cast into fiery oil.... *or the boiler of the train.*

What do they feed this thing? Bones? Are we going to all die just to keep this train running?

The black storm rolls on restraints, chained to the ground while churning rage into the sky, smoking a living pipe of prayer.

I remember reading how peace pipes represent the smoke carrying prayers to Creator. This train is that, but louder than thunder as it roars across the Tay Bridge, snorting rage at being restricted to the earth on a single track when it was destined for freedom.

Knocking makes me squeal in loud fright, the whizzing of the world beyond the window shackling me with vertigo when dizziness spirals me around by a tense hand locked to my arm.

"Are you all right?"

"P...erfect."

Why is Mr Black in my suite? Has half an hour vanished already?

"I heard you scream when I knocked. My apologies, I thought something was amiss."

"Spider," I lie, needing to start behaving like a coherent adult in possession of all faculties.

Low level chuckling whispers softly into my ear canal from the wide open space of empty standing next to me, imbuing me with a severe case of the heebie jeebies. With me in the clutches of a paranoid convulsion, Mr Black releases my arm as if he caused the involuntary reflex.

And that makes me feel bad but doesn't stop me from looking guiltily behind me for the joker. There's probably a hidden camera in here. Are we some kind of social experiment? Would it look funny if I bathed in my bra and knickers? I don't fancy some creep peeking down a lens at my privates.

Ghostly breath gasps heavily in my ear and I flinch, my skin turning into gigantic cobbles of fear-fever. It's the kind of breathing you expect from your stalker down the phone line at midnight, not from fresh air.

"Are you cold?" says Black conversationally, using logic as a ward for my irrational reaction.

"A little," I nod. Stilted awkwardness is rapidly infiltrating this situation.

Movement in my periphery crushes my fib with eight slender legs tenting across the double bed in all their hair glory.

Jumping behind Black, I squeak, "Spider!"

My god it's bigger than Black's hand.

Quaking in full on freak out mode, I cringe in the corner, expecting to be rescued, but he looks paler than crematorium ash at the sight of the hairy beast.

Moving at quantum speed to plan B, I start screaming crimson murder at the top of my lungs until Molly the mannequin comes rushing in.

Halting abruptly, smoothing down her jacket, she gives Black the chastising stare of disapproval at his presence in my quarters, and then follows the trajectory of me pointing an outstretched arm from a safe distance, jabbing my appendage at the monster like a flag of surrender.

"Sorry about this Miss Dubois, I'll help this chap off our esteemed carriage." And just like that the demented woman scoops up the hairy predator and pops him into her pocket as if he's no more than a teatime snack to be scoffed like an eataholic in the broom closet when no one is about.

Calmly exiting my envelope of luxury she inclines her head like she's the royalty here, still giving Black the accusing glare.

The brush of a cobweb pressures a trace down my cheek and I wave my arms about frantically, doing the spider dance. Nothing is there, of course. Since being here I feel like a mental patient waiting to meet a bondage expert who can introduce me to the joys of rubber.

Freaks! This place has people that are just ... this has to be a joke.

Looking around again I narrow my gaze, trying to locate the hidden camera, running my hand over the polished veneer of mahogany panels set out like picture frames.

Do they open? Is something else going to crawl in here through a convenient panel operated by Dr Jekyll?

I knew something was off.

"You okay?"

"No! No, I'm bleedin' not okay," I snap, verging on hysterical. Stopping my search, I glower at Black, "Why are you in my suite?"

"Oh, er, just wanted to compare them really. You have a double bed and I have two singles. They must like you."

The fright has worn off and with it so has the adrenaline, forcing me to sit with suddenly weak knees on the chair opposite the dressing table. "They don't even know me. Why are we here?"

"Funny you should mention that, I was going to ask you the same thing."

"Right, well if you've concluded your business could I have some privacy please?" I say, lifting my chin and giving him the female 'no nonsense' pointed stare.

"Of course, yes, I was just leaving anyway." He shadows the walls with his tall frame in three steps, moves across the threshold, and lifts his hand in a weak "Taahra."

Once the door is closed I check my wristwatch. I have ten minutes to be presentable for all the toffs in the lounge, I'll just have to search this place later.

Diving for the bathroom with my handbag, I unwind the scarf, daring to expose my neck to the psychic vampires aboard the ghost train, and scoot off my shoes, sitting down on the toilet lid to wipe the wetness out of my pumps with toilet paper.

Oh god!

The tissue comes away bright red, the shade of whore hotpants, and I drop the court shoe to turn my foot upside down, wriggling like a contortionist because of my pencil skirt.

Argh!

Hiking it up to my hips I sit down again, putting my foot on my knee like a rugby player about to have a celebratory beer. Delicately dabbing at the underside of my foot I spot a neat line scoring the pad behind my big toe, suctioning the tights to my sole in clotting grossness.

Great! *Just* what I need. I don't have any plasters and if that bleeds again my shoe's going to squeak like I forgot to oil my hip.

Wiping out my shoe, I stand, yanking down my pantyhose, balling it up and stuffing it into the dollhouse sized bin behind the loo, and then carefully line the inside of my shoe with toilet paper.

Fab! Smoothing my skirt back down I just have time to reapply lipstick and repin my hair before dashing to make the deadline in the lounge coach.

Grabbing open the door I rush out, just to turn around and bullet back in, looking around in panic. Is my bag safe here? Do I have to take it with me? Are any of these people trustworthy? I mean if we *are* part of a social experiment wouldn't I illustrate just how monumentally stupid women are if they leave their toiletries and documents unattended for some wanker to jerk off into your shampoo or something? And then try on my perfume and eat that old stale mint in the bottom of my bag? Or take that emergency stash of dosh out the hidden pocket? Or...

"You coming or what?"

Pegging around with the speed of Jet Li, I face the endlessly snooping Black. "What do you want?"

He taps his wrist neatly hidden under a jacket sleeve, "Tick tock Crumpet, time's a wasting."

He doesn't have his toiletries with him. What was I thinking? They'll call me eccentric and three cherries short of a fruitcake.

I have to pull myself together.

"Any more spiders?" he smiles congenially.

"Don't even tempt fate or I'll put a voodoo doll covered in crabs in your bed. Got it?"

"I'm betting you're single."

"You'd bet right," I snap, following him out of my room and into the cramped yet opulent vintage passage.

I've got a bad feeling about all of this.

Chapter 2

Following Black, we emerge into a Tetris assembled rendition of a lounge, long and narrow and overrun with two very bland combinations of blue and heather-purple.

Crowding the quarters with over the top extras are pelmets and curtains on each window, which somehow manage to choke the room with an innocuous noose of oppression.

Didn't they ever think a skylight would be a good idea on a train? Instead they have fans of bronze, and dark – (depression masquerading as posh) – wood down the centre of the roof, stuck in a swamp of glossy white Victorian wallpaper, framed with two support beams and hideous tulip lights.

If this is what wealthy looks like I quite fancy myself as a commoner. Less is clearly more. They could use blinds made out of gold for all I care, but for Thor's sake let some light in here.

The imbued decrepit loony aunt vibe makes me want to hold my breath for fear of catching the plague from the other patrons.

Molly waits dead centre with her fake smile and plastic complexion, observing us as we unobtrusively duck into velvet chairs, quietly watching and waiting for the grand madam to spin her magic.

"Now that we've all congregated I'd like to formally welcome you aboard. You will discover buckets of champagne placed strategically throughout the car, please help yourselves, relax, and celebrate our five star accommodation." She turns, pointing to a zigzag passage, "Beyond this car is the observation carriage. If you smoke, please refrain from lighting up inside. The observation car has a railed section outdoors where you can enjoy the fresh air from the back of the train. You will find a container placed specifically to collect cigarette butts next to the door. Do not flick your filters into the countryside, to do so would violate our hospitality and we will stop the train and you will disembark immediately, no matter where we are at any given time."

Black irises deepen to pitch as she skewers us all with her stare, "Do I make myself clear?"

I bet she wears tons of latex when she's off duty.

Everyone nods, murmuring agreement, so I respectfully do my part. I thought the royal train didn't have rules. What if they have a guest who smokes? Are they going to drop the King of Venus off in middle earth just because he lit up his cherry tobacco pipe after stuffing his gills with gourmet cuisine?

A skinny man who looks like he's drowning in his jacket timidly puts his hand up, like a child asking permission to pee.

"Yes, Mr Jones?" snaps Molly.

"Why are we here?" he mumbles, visibly shrinking with all eyes on him.

Dominatrix Molly gives him her sadistic smile, "I'll leave that to the Captain to disclose. You will have after dinner drinks with him this evening."

Turning back to include us in her all-encompassing authority, she says, "Dinner is promptly served at six-thirty. Do not be late."

Snapping her fingers, a bellhop type dude rushes forward, giving her a wooden box.

"In here I have pocket watches. Please use them during your stay to keep time for meals as we've found the magnetic interference from the train tracks derails most modern time pieces. So dinner is when both hands of the watch are on the number six. That will be all."

Was that supposed to be train humour? L-a-m-e. *Derails*, she's derailed, clearly.

Inclining her head as if she's done with her interviews of the working class for the day, her majesty sashays back the way we came, leaving in her wake a stiff silence.

Bellhop minions after her like a jester eager to please mistress and the train's whistle blows again as if she just reached the captain to crack her whip into his sweaty broken body bowed in subservience over the controls, shackled on his knees so her cat-o-nine-tails connects perfectly every time.

Its whistle isn't cheery or wailing this time, but a long suffering keen let loose from Pandora's box. It's grief steam mingling a lethal cocktail with hazardous smoke.

Well... that would explain my time lapse. Maybe I'm sensitive to magnetic fields or something?

Lanky gets up and jerks his thumb in the direction of the observation car, "I'm going for a fag then."

And like lemmings the morons all stand and shuffle after him. Not that I can blame them as this carriage *is* downright stifling.

"Shall we?" asks Black, giving me his polite smile and offering me his elbow.

Do men think women are that feeble we can't walk unless we have a man to use as a lamppost? Lurching on muscle to assist us the way a marm uses a cane? Didn't he notice Manic Molly? She wouldn't need a man to lean on, she'd probably shatter his kneecaps for even implying it.

Maybe Black is simply embracing the courtesy of the bygone era we're currently inhabiting. I bet he doesn't offer his arm to the inebriated slag down the pub.

"Yeah, whatever..." I grumble, standing, pointedly ignoring his offer to support myself on him like an invalid.

Gentry is overrated and insinuated condescending chauvinism. Acting this way is bonkers because rightly we should only link arms with lovers and good friends.

Or maybe I'm just full of shit.

If I said any of this out loud he'd mumble, "I take it you're single then?"

Wally.

Oddly he's a likeable enough fellow. He guides us through to the next car, going so far as to do the five finger punch at the base of my back... the way men do. Seriously are we all woozy, or alcoholics, that we need that extra hand to keep us steady and upright and moving in the right direction?

Does it make them feel superior by silently implying we're all ditzy idiots with a mallet's sense of direction?

I feel like tripping him so he hits his head on this vastly impractical split screen to the observation car.

It's not made for fatties, that's for sure. I saw one man here who could easily get stuck in this like a whale in a turnstile.

Flopping into the nearest mint green chair as we breach into the next coach, the velvet heat of it chafes the back of my naked legs. It's horrid the way they've used these thick fabrics that were made to smother heretics. It's too much! Maybe I was Japanese in my last life because I'm pining for wide open minimalist space. Natural, light, zen-ish stuff made of natural fibres instead of this cloying and cluttered prison on wheels.

Black saunters to the other end to look through the glass at the rejects outside sucking on their vices. I bet Manic Molly sucks on her vices too.

I can't imagine what would possess anyone to go out on the viewing deck. It goes against my survival instincts to step outside on a moving train.

So now what? How long before dinner? Do we have to dress formally or something?

Damn, I forgot to get a pocket-watch.

Struggling to get out of the possessive suction of the chair I ungraciously force myself out the way a toddler would scrambling out of a blow up paddling pool.

Frazzled from the armchair wrestle I escape to the next car.

June 1. Chair 0.

Marching up to the box, I flip the lid open and select a small nurse sized watch, slipping it into my pocket just as a cold breeze wheezes down my blouse collar.

Shivering I twist about, triple checking I'm alone, looking for open windows and air vents.

The scenery outside is nice. We're already travelling across lush countryside, verdant with tweeds and various shades of hessian. I'm about to wander over for a gander when my solace is intruded upon.

"Miss Dubois, I have a question for you," says Black, as he meanders back my way looking jaunty with hands buried in his pockets. All he's missing is Hyde Park and a newspaper under his arm.

"Yes?" I snark, wondering why he can't make any new friends.

He must be a Cling-on.

I am so tempted to hold up the Vulcan V in salute. Bet he spends entire weekends playing video games and forgets to change his underwear.

"Why do you have toilet paper sticking out of your shoe?" he muses, giving me no escape as the offensive article is bang in the cross-hairs of his amused stare.

Oh bollocks! The effing paper must have moved when I walked.

Heating up like I just stuck my finger in a live socket, I give him my chagrined smirk, "I like to make a statement. Who wants to be forgettable?"

"Aaah," he mutters, his smile unsure, raising his eyebrows at me as if he's scandalised again.

Stick around buddy, I assure you I'll manage to permanently disfigure your sense of decorum.

Strutting to a nearby chair, I sit down and point at the box, "Don't forget to select your time piece."

The second his back is turned I start poking my finger around the edge of my shoe, burying the bloody bog roll back where it belongs.

"Good lord! It's six already! We'd better get a move on!" he exclaims. He does it with enough emotion you'd swear we get beheaded if we're late.

Heaven help us if we keep double six waiting.... ooooh... drama queen.

"Of course, we wouldn't want to be the insurgents who dare to challenge punctuality," I say sarcastically, staring pointedly at him, resisting the strong urge to hold the loser L up on my forehead. "The regent royal won't be attending dinner, darling. No need to get your knickers in a twist."

He gives me that 'you're queer' look again.

Screwing up my eyes in answer I walk in front of him, knowing that by the time I reach my door the toilet paper will be sticking up behind my heel and my shoe will probably squeak.

How it managed to get from the front of my shoe to the back is anyone's guess. Royalty obviously qualifies for Houdini bog roll. Wipe your bum for too long and it might nest in there and start multiplying.

Black tries to rush my model composure along in his flap at being late for dinner, but I refuse to budge.

"Sorry Crumpet, just going to come past you quickstix."

And he shoves around me, leaving me lurching for real this time into the antiquated veneer of the passage, watching Black run away like James May.

The urge to pee comes on strong watching him run. It's hilarious! James May doesn't run, he Charlie Chaplin's his way, and it makes Black look camper than the queens of New Orleans.

Doing the knees locked walk before my bladder bursts, my shoe starts to squeal, but I don't care, I'm weeping with laughter, using the wall to shimmy along to my own room.

Maybe Victorian women just needed to wee-wee badly? Hence the need for an arm to wiggle next to while cramping up her thighs.

My arm madam?

Why yes please kind sir.

I thought so Charlotte, you're looking peeved.

Because I need to urinate George, and I'm not wearing my padded bloomers under this bustle today.

Not to worry Charlotte I shall lend you my arm, I am your gallant support in your moment of need.

Oh George, how would I ever get on without you?

You'd be piqued a lot, Charlotte.

But George, I rather like it when you pique in the formal rose garden, under my pantaloons.

Hush now Charlotte, or I'll destroy your reputation by letting you piss your pants right here.

Giggling, I shunt open my door and duck walk to the bathroom.

Chapter 3

I keep checking the special time warp pocket-watch so I won't be late. Deciding to err on the side of caution I have made an effort for dinner and am wearing my Christmas dress of velvet so dark the blue looks black.

It also makes me look taller and more slender, but the heels which match are no joke. You could stab someone to death with them.

Securing the space continuum equaliser timepiece on my pendant, I take one last peek at the mirror above the dressing table, situated conveniently right next to the door, and open the door to make haste to the dining car.

As if he's been loitering with his ear to the keyhole Mr Black exits his suite at the same moment with a dramatic whoosh.

Locking the door, he gives me a grin, "Perfect timing, what."

And the blasted man offers me his elbow again.

Sigh.

Gritting my teeth I walk awkwardly next to him, in too little space for two people to comfortably stroll side by side. Off we shuffle like geriatrics, all the while my ridiculous stilettos thorn into the pile in nerve sawing hacks.

If anyone asks, this is how Cinderella lost that slipper.

I'm having to bunch my toes to increase the tension in my shoes to prevent the carpet from keeping the shoe as I step. Every minute struggle is a hacking battle of my ability to keep my shoe while the heel tip wants to stay imbedded in the blasted carpet. In one foul sweep a man can reduce a graceful maiden into a gnarly hunchback.

Walk swiftly and we glide, make us dribble down the passage and we're all rigid while we wage war with design flaws.

At least we find out the purpose of this sojourn after dinner.

With my escort we arrive at the dining car, which has tables for two sporadically placed down either side of its length.

It's dinner detention.

I've noticed something about these carpets and it annoys the OCD freak in me. It has a join down the centre, mismatching the pattern, and it irks me as surely as halitosis.

Come on, surely with their budget they could have forked out the money to lay a plaid carpet without a seam down the middle? We stare at it when we walk, we just can't help it.

A tall and weathered man steps forward, inclining his balding head with long thin strands of grey clinging to his forehead and worn so long in the back it peppers his jacket collar with rats tails.

He's dressed like a stage coach driver right out of the 1920's. Even the cut of his shirt and jacket is uniform to the era. Give him a dusty top hat and his ensemble would be complete. His shirt has the distinct stain of tobacco and age imbedded in it, the collar is the kind which doesn't allow a tie with an edge ever so slightly frayed... like my nerves.

He gives me a thin-lipped grin, elongating his narrow face and long chin, his pearly whites turned tortoiseshell with longevity and abuse.

Weirdo.

"Right this way," he gestures, and we trail after him to a reserved table where our names are scrawled on cards left in waiting.

Black allows me to go first so I can move like a human and not a mutant this time. Head up, I do 'the walk' to my chair.

He'd better not be staring at my arse.

It seems we've been segregated consecutively to our arrival. Mr Black and myself are stuck at a little table at a window as we were the last to join the party on the train.

The miniscule window holds back brocade curtains with tasselled cord, and I clench my jaw while being subjected to having the waiter hold out my chair for me.

I've never been very good at receiving chivalry with grace. This is a song and dance for the fortunate, not a working girl like me.

Copying Mr Black I unfold the burgundy (dried blood) napkin, and place it with genteel finesse across my lap.

"Our first course this evening is a piquant heirloom sundried tomato terrine, with a hint of scotch bonnet. The tomatoes were steeped in a pomegranate oil and juice decoction to enhance their ripe robust flavour before slowly simmering in oak aged red wine. Will you be joining the other diners in the set menu?"

Black nods at 'Dickens' who looks better dressed to serve the hearse than dinner. I follow suit, amicably agreeing to whatever goes. Best to get the lay of the protocol before becoming difficult.

"Very good. This evening's wine is a speciality Bordeaux from the maternal region in France. Of course it was introduced to France by the Romans and it's with reverence that we serve such a noble bouquet to accompany tonight's gastronomical delights," says Dickens, bowing as he scuffles backwards with hands neatly clasped behind his back as if he's just copped the skeleton key to the World Bank from Black's dinner jacket pocket.

What an eccentric character.

Black smiles at me when Dickens scarpers, "This place gets weirder and weirder."

A strange dude sitting four tables behind Black is giving me the oogly eye. He looks like an overweight Greek chef with a tight cap of grey curls stacked in a topiary on the top of his head.

"Henri? Are you even hearing a word I say?" says the lady in front of him, sitting with her back to us.

He does the 'I can't breathe I smoke too much' wheeze when he glares at her, "Mildred, I may be old but I'm not deaf yet."

So he's French? I swear they can sniff out my DNA at twenty paces. Sometimes I hate that I'm unmarried. I can't wait to lose this surname and start over. It doesn't matter where I am, if there is a Frenchman in the vicinity he'll find me and come onto me.

Shooting my withering scowl at him I return my attention to Black, "Yes, the waiter certainly looks.... theatrical."

"Wine?" he asks, lifting the decanter set on the table.

"Please," I nod. "I think I'll need a few glasses to sleep on a moving train."

"Oh no," he shakes his head, while pouring a generous measure for each of us. "This train usually parks overnight while the passengers slumber. That's part of its allure as a five star deluxe mode of transport. Our comfort is paramount."

Oh yeah? Then I'd like to move to a new cabin because mine is haunted.

Lifting his glass, he implies I should do the same.

Copying him again I lift the crystal stem, examining the gold trim catching the soft lighting in the dining car the way a filling in a pirate's smile lights up at a bonfire.

He gives it a whiff with flared nostrils, then says intimately as if trying not to be overheard teaching me wine etiquette, "Your first sip should be small, hold it in your mouth for ten seconds before swallowing. Swirl it around a bit, this allows the layers of the bouquet to make themselves known. This smells like it has a delicate but robust palate, with a hint of chilli and raspberry, maybe even a touch of chocolate. Okay, go..."

Pretentious much?

He takes a sip, looking like he has toothache with the faces he makes while mouthwashing teeth staining tannins around his gob.

Sampling the red stuff, I hold it up to the light. It coats the inside of the glass as if it has sugar in it. Maybe they sweeten it without telling anyone? Maybe it's off? Watered down with soured fruit juice most probably.

Leaving it to sit on my tongue, it becomes too potent and nasty so I swallow quickly, tempted to grimace with the aftertaste. It's borderline vile. It's thick and warm, leaving a sharp tang in my throat which makes me want to cough. Choking, I fight back the eye watering. I do not need to ruin my make-up over an exorbitant sip of Beelzebub juice.

"Hmmm, wines of this pedigree are rare. It has the consistency and taste of a very mature wine. I wonder what vintage it is?"

Give me a mojito or Cosmopolitan over this any day. I don't care how vintage it is, it's putrid.

"Who cares," I shrug, putting my glass back on the white linen just as two steaming plates are placed in front of us.

Dickens gives us his Riffraff smile and skitters off doing the stick insect walk. He's shifty. He dropped the bowls as fast as he could and put space between us and him as if underneath the lid of each terrine is a smoke bomb ready to gas us into eternal sleep.

Suspicious, I cautiously pry open the fragile lid, looking at a pond of blood red soup in a dam of white bone china.

So what did they hide in here? Scorpions?

Leaving the lid on my side plate I pick up the spoon and dowse for hidden horrors.

A hairy man hand clamps over mine and Black whispers, "That's the dessert spoon." Releasing my hand he taps the table as if chastising a little child, "This is the one you want."

It's just a spoon, who cares which one I use, it all goes in the same hole.

Ignoring rules of engagement I continue clanging the metal around the bowl to find the submersed eyeball. Satisfied there's nothing dodgy lurking within, I sample it.

My throat closes, my eyes start watering uncontrollably, and sweat blisters my temples.

Bleedin' heck!

Suffocating on 'a hint of scotch bonnet' I discard my standards and guzzle the congealed wine.

Waves of nausea swell over my ribcage and I dry heave into the napkin now clamped over my mouth.

"It's got no chloroform in it so inhaling vapours from the napkin won't help I'm afraid. Do you need your smelling salts dear?" jokes Black.

Not daring to respond I wait for my insides to settle before dabbing at my eyes and slumping in my chair, wishing for fresh air and zero ambient motion. Maybe it's travel sickness?

"Not preggers are you?" pries the nosy man.

"No," I grumble, my fire missing in the aftermath of the toxic soup attack.

Sullen, I watch Black methodically consume his soup the posh way, scooping the spoon on the opposite side of the terrine.

That's always struck me as stupid. Who decided it was wrong to spoon close to you when eating something runny? Masochists like Manic Molly are the kinds of people who make up daft social rules like that just so they have an excuse to cane impressionable young children during their formative years. Slotting them neatly into a system of unquestioning surrender.

And people still think zombies aren't real. Ha.

That, or it's a stupid line drawn to discern who is a 'winner' and who is a 'loser' on the societal chessboard. As if eating a bowl of soup could truly elevate anyone above others, puhlease. This is my problem with old money, they're a bunch of condescending fucktards with children who single-handedly keep the drug barons in business.

This isn't my cup of tea, not one bit. I'd rather be eating spring rolls and chips out on the pier, in the fresh air and wind. With my fingers!

"So..." says Black.

"So," I mimic.

He pushes his emptied plate away, the red ridges left behind look like blood spatter striating the porcelain.

"Do you have a first name, Miss Dubois?"

"June," I offer up, hating that complete strangers feel they have the right to know everything about you. Single? Preggers? Name?

Would you like a retina scan and pap smear too?

"I'm Martin," he smiles, offering his hand over the table for me to shake in formal greeting.

"How do you do," I sneer in my queen intonation, shaking the hand with my dead fish rendition of a shake.

It always freaks people out when you do the limp handshake.

"Impressive grip," he laughs, releasing my hand as if I picked my nose before clasping his.

Gotcha!

"Mmm," I mumble noncommittally.

Dickens appears like a phantom materialising, becoming more solid and stinky as his shadow grows enough to slant over the crisp linen of the table. It's like watching the time exposure of bacteria multiplying in a petri dish.

"Was the terrine not to your liking?" He's giving me a 'the captain will hear of this treason' stare.

"Um... no." I give him my flat defiant smile. "And could I have a glass of water please? I don't like wine."

Arching a cynical eyebrow he looks at me as if I haven't a shred of culture in my body, but I'd beg to differ. I've heard we breed an entire circus between just our eyelashes. I'd hate to know what festers under toenails when we're not looking. I mean, I did bleed all over the inside of my shoe, surely that counts for some kind of culture? Penicillin it won't be, but I'm useful for a plethora of breeding opportunities without being 'preggers'.

"Of course," he bows stiffly, clanging Black's plate onto mine in a display of disapproval and temper.

Watching the highwayman jerk away doing his grasshopper imitation, I heave a sigh and stare at my reflection in the window darkened by night.

"You're in shit with Sherlock," whispers Black.

"No shit, Sherlock," I smirk, glancing at him, finally cracking a smile.

"So... what do you do?" he pries some more.

"What do *you* do?" I counter, annoyed with twenty questions. If I was sitting here with Chris Tarrant I'd only have to answer fifteen *and* be a million quid richer.

"A bit of this and a bit of that," he evades.

"What a coincidence, me too," I smile, doing what I am sure is an award winning copy of Molly's. It's the 'eat shit and shut up' teeth snarl.

And bang on cue Dickens brings his gangrene cologne over to us again, placing two plates in front of us with precocious domes smuggling the contents.

Turning, he snatches a glass of water from the jester minion and slams it onto the crimson tablecloth before stomping off back to the car next door where all the food is waiting on heated thingamabobs.

Oogly eye is watching me again and I'm so tempted to salute him with my middle finger. And I do – because life is too short to be polite to leery assholes who gawk, especially when they're sitting with Mrs Leery at the time.

"Do you like my French manicure?" I say a little too loud to Black, overtly extending my middle finger.

"You're not a people person, are you?"

"Whatever gave you that impression?" I half giggle under my breath, dropping my voice again, "Just telling that old fart to sod off. He keeps staring."

Black twists to scowl disapproval at the old gent who immediately moves his full focus to his filet mignon. Turning back to me Black offers a conspiratorial wink and flamboyantly lifts the lid off dinner.

Two very rare beef medallions sit next to steaming beetroot, and a purple cabbage-tomato chutney. It smells like liver, immediately curdling my nose with haemoglobin stench.

"May I?" he offers to take the lid off my plate too, and I nod.

Depositing the domes on the floor, he lifts his knife and fork and slices into the meat without hesitation. I watch the flesh squelch under the pressure, bleeding out its centre to coalesce a fatty skein of sacrifice on the virginal porcelain.

Popping the portion into his mouth, he's scoffing away looking like he's in carnivore nirvana when he suddenly stops to savagely point his knife at me, "Aren't you eating?"

"I'm a vegetarian," I shrug, my stomach doing the jive at watching him consume the haemorrhaging morsel which is secreting bloodied juice over his lip.

Grinning with a full mouth, he ducks his head under the table, pops back up as if surprising a toddler with peekaboo, and says with a bulging cheek, "Not fair, you're wearing a long skirt."

"Aren't you a bit old to be peeping up skirts?" I counter.

"You're one of those hairy legged carpet munchers, are you?" he muffles around masticating.

"Do you get called an assuming stereotypical prick often?" I snap.

"So you're not into girls and communes and wild strap-on threesomes?" he smirks, carving off another chunk of beef.

"My preferences are my business, not yours."

"Aha! So I'm right! Did Martin put you off men, darling?"

This time I show *him* my middle finger, "Fuck you, Martin Dubois."

"Ah, but you wouldn't, would you?" he winks, nearly choking in pompous guffaws at his wit. "I'm not your speed. Maybe when I get a bit older and develop some hairy manboobs."

"You are so gross!"

"I do my best," he winks again.

"You mean your worst," I lobby back.

The ominous shadow turning our table into a dark shrine to Molech shuts us both up to stare at Dickens.

"*Now* what is the problem, Miss Dubois?" he sneers at me down his squiff and pointy nose.

"Look, er..." Cripes I nearly called him Dickens. "...mister uhm, could I just go straight to dessert?"

Black pipes up, "She's backwards, she'd have loved the entire meal if she'd started at the finish line. Then she would have licked that delicacy off the plate."

The moron gives me a wink again, and yes I get his snide humour but I'm coming perilously close to wanting to deck the smug twat off his chair.

Idiot.

"Certainly," grimaces Dickens, as if he just got a pube caught in the elastic of his y-fronts.

Lifting my plate he honestly looks like he considers dumping it over my head before withdrawing to the mysterious carriage next door.

"Now you've done it. There'll be a public hearing now. They'll stop the train and make you walk home."

"Shut up, Black," I snap, irritation riding me hard.

"Black? I'm not black."

Oh crumbs!

"Uhm, it's my nickname for you. Everyone gets one on first meeting," I explain, giving him an ingratiating shrug.

"But you knew on first meeting I'm Dubois."

"Yes, but I can't call you Dubois because it sounds like I'm talking to myself! I may seem barmy but being mental is not on my bucket list," I argue.

I'm perfectly rational, I just don't come across that way.

"Oh, right," he says, suddenly deflated and sitting back in his chair, somehow having devoured most of his meal between our slams of conversation. "Call me Martin, then."

"No."

"Why not?" he insists, leaning forward in rapt attention.

I *am* a social experiment, I knew it. Is he the resident shrink here to evaluate the subjects in the case study?

"My ex is Martin, and if I call you Martin I'll end up wanting to punch your teeth in every time I say your name."

He sits back, aghast, dropping his cutlery, gonging the plate with a loud clatter.

Is it because I dated a Martin? What, do they all stick together or something? Or does he think I have a subliminal and pathological attraction to anyone with the name?

Everyone in the dining car looks our way and I wish I could just slide down in my seat and behave like an ingrate, but I'm putting on the show of my life here so lift my chin marginally higher and hold the poise.

"So you're not lesbian?"

Thanks Black, now everyone is *definitely* staring at me. The silence in here is deafening even with the rhythmic click-clack of wheels on a track.

I kick him under the table, hard.

Yelping, the vein in his forehead pops out while Dickens lunges toward us in the leper walk to bang a red crème caramel type thingy in front of me. His force is such that it wobbles with seizures as he lopes away, saying nothing this time.

Picking up the 'soup' spoon I prod the gelatinous blob.

Black grunts while rubbing his shin, "What the effin hell did you do that for?"

"Thanks to you I've just become a public spectacle."

"Who cares what other people assume, we're having a civilised conversation here."

"Just shut it and eat your dinner." To emphasise my point I slice a blob of bright crimson custard off the mound and dump it into my mouth so I can't converse with anyone.

Brutal citrus zest burns up my nose, watering my eyes again and eliciting a quick coughing hack into my fist.

"Well? Is it any good?" he asks, leaning closer to inspect the icing sugar snowflaking the plate.

"They need to sack the chef on this train," I whisper hoarsely, rinsing my mouth out with water.

Black acts like an old friend of longstanding when he picks up his dessert spoon and slices off a quenelle of my pudding, sucking it into his mouth with the precision of a nipple connoisseur.

"That's all right actually," he nods approval.

Shoving my plate across the table for him to finish, I state, "You have the constitution of a meteor."

"Never met one," he mumbles with his gob full. The melting brûlée coating his tongue embosses his mouth with the look of a vampire who just broke a carotid open.

The wet blood look bleeding onto his lip somersaults my stomach and I lurch out of my chair, stumbling for the exit in lethal shoes.

I'm going to be sick.

Why was everything red? What were we really eating?

Bile volcanoes up my insides and I vault for the powder room, all the while a cold tentacle has a firm grip on my nape as if trying to assure me I'm not alone here, he'll rub my back while I throw up.

Blanketed in cold ripples, panic perspires a frost of fear into my temples and armpits. Rushing past the mirror in the ladies I see a distinct entity shadowing me, close enough to share my aura.

Banging the lid up, collapsing onto my knees, retching uncontrollably, my posture is that of the devout praying for absolution after offending the chef.

If Manic Molly hears about this there'll be hell to pay, I'm sure.

No, not hell... penance.

Chapter 4

As I exit the powder room I'm faced with the two sources of retribution standing side by side. Molly and Dickens are glowering at me as if I publicly masturbated in the dining car and ran out to fetch my nipple clamps.

"What?" I snap, in no mood to be accountable to complete strangers on petty ego trips.

"Are you all right?" asks Molly, even employing a concerned inflection into her tone.

If she was an actress she'd win a Bafta every year, and no doubt be inflated with herself.

"No," I grumble, wishing they'd step aside so I can escape the firing squad.

"Was it the pudding?" asks Dickens, the sweat on his head causing the mangy scalp to ooze with a fermented discharge.

The man smells like toe-jam, contaminating the air with medieval hygiene. I take a prudent step away from him.

"What was that stuff?" I demand, beginning to feel confrontational. I'm in the mood to cause a stink.

"Blood oranges flown in from California and turned into a dense pannacotta by Chef Bau," he explains, looking for all intents and purposes like I offended his snootiness.

Well I think Chef Bau sucks, and for the record ask guests if they have allergies or aversions before putting weeping flesh on a plate under their nose. I can still smell it even after spewing my guts.

"If you'll excuse me," I say, lifting my head the way a cat does when it's ignoring you.

Verbalising none of my inner dialogue I hightail it back into the dining car just to find the place utterly deserted.

Where the heck is everybody? Did Spock beam in or something? Shouldn't the train's whistle blow if we're experiencing the rapture. I mean, come on, it wasn't my fault I was puking when the pious were reaped.

I glance silent condemnation at the circumspect devil and her henchman.

"Carry on to the observation car," nods Molly, her order leaving no room to broach argument. "Captain McMorain is waiting there, we're serving cheese and wine for after dinner."

McMorain? I've never heard of a surname so clearly polarised.

All right.

Giving Molly a mirror copy of her polite smile, I continue walking to the next room using every ounce of ballet training I received in the childhood years of gruelling torture wherein I endured to walk bottom in, head up, shoulders relaxed, and all this contortion accomplished with physic's defying fluid grace.

Entering into the next car, which I immediately note has been rearranged for the auspicious occasion, the accumulation of life instils a fair amount of relief.

Aged mustard drapes are still open to vacuum cold night air into the carriage, the viewing pen exposed and occupied by two shadowy smokers, flowers flutter in breezed agitation next to spearmint-velvet settees, and the past tartan champions in Earl Grey hued frames are boldly on display as the seating currently leaves the walls accessible.

The dried-blood brocade wallpaper matches the blood clot pattern in the carpet, the hue more of a communist-baked-brick used to smash a skull in. It holds the faint speckle of an unclean bludgeon left to rust a little before being sheathed.

In fact, this entire train thing feels like a bunch of narrow coffins coupled together and stuck onto harnessed wheels, yoked together in metal penitentiary like slaves joined by their collars.

"Ah, Miss Dubois I presume?" booms a deep manly baritone while I attempt to pick a spot to park my derriere.

Snapping my focus on the man while apprehension bargains for my afterlife, I can't believe the driver-captain dude is wearing a kilt. Surely that's impractical? Jeans didn't become globally popular because of the fine weave of its cotton but because of its durability and practicality, and I'm sure he doesn't need to dress like they picked him up from the Destiny Stone when no one but the staff see him at work?

It makes me want to yell 'O captain my captain', but I doubt anyone here would appreciate my teasing.

Nodding nervously at the barrier clearly making his purposeful way toward me, I notice Black waving me over to sit next to him with a dose of gratitude.

Scooting to Black I plonk down quickly, taking the offered plate of cheese and crackers with an appreciative smirk. "You're a lifesaver," I whisper to him.

"I know," he mutters, giving me his signature wink. "I feel like I keep saving you from yourself."

Captain McMorain slots himself onto the arm of my settee, cornering me between him and Black most effectively.

"I'm McMorain," he smiles in sinister cunning, offering his hand for me to shake.

I do, quickly, too nervous to use the limp routine, and quickly withdraw my hand to survey the others.

"June..." Bushy eyebrows pull together like a tightening strap and he gives me a soul penetrating black eyed stare, "May I call you June?"

"Sure," I mumble, precariously balancing an expensive plate laden with cheese and crackers, shooting a grin at Black, "It's better than calling me May."

"Well June..." he continues as if I didn't just drop a funny.

I suppose it is only amusing if you have the inside joke – which only I'm privy to.

"...I've called this gathering to explain the purpose of your journey. Contrary to popular belief this is not The Royal Scotsman, but the Moonshine Express. It belonged to a very powerful moonraker named Dubois. Anton Dubois."

He pauses to give me a meaningful stare.... it's expectant.

What does he want me to say? It's purely coincidental I'm sure.

Black starts nibbling from his own plate of cheese delicacies and I see it as an escape, dastardly copying him. Shovelling morsels into my mouth the way McMorain's men shovel coal into the furnace, I just stare back, urging him to go on with a perfunctory nod.

McMorain pats my knee in a patronising manner, leaning down to speak intimately to me like we're on our first date, "I'm sure you are aware that Anton is a Roman name."

Two black eyebrows pop up while he waits insistently for an answer, his face too close, his eyes glossy like newly tapped oil wells.

Shrinking back into the velvet of the settee, my velvet dress rubs the pile the wrong way and I feel like I'm being velcroed into place.

Swallowing a sharp cheddar, I mumble, "No, I didn't know."

"It means *beyond praise*," informs Black, joining the conversation which I'm clearly late to. I missed all the good stuff and now I have remedial one on one time with the man himself.

"Or *priceless*, and *inestimable*," adds McMorain.

"I don't follow why his name is such a big deal," I contest while they spew useless information like geeks comparing IQ's, or jocks with the measuring tape out.

"His name gives you a clue. Anton broke laws, he did as he pleased, he was a leader, a pioneer, a rebel. The man had the kind of charisma which starts cults and has the spineless swearing allegiance and signing in blood on the dotted line without ever asking for details. He cared not for the system but chose instead to carve his own fate in the stars." Patting my knee again and leaving his hand conspicuously on it, McMorain says obtusely, "That's where you come in, June."

Lifting another cracker to occupy my mandibles, I bang elbows with Black. Hemmed in, I'm beginning to feel stifled.

Glancing between them, it strikes me as strange how they seem to resemble each other. Identical dark eyes, wavy jet hair that's so shiny it could be sculpted with Brill cream, and even the shape of their eyebrows is the same. Black just looks like a younger version of McMorain.

McMorain has the heavy set look of a man who isn't afraid to haul the recently deceased and dig graves in the dead of night for his loot of corpses. He's clearly no stranger to physical strain whereas Black appears to be the professor type who spends his time lifting books instead.

"June..." says the Captain, detaching his hand from my thigh and adjusting his kilt pin ever so slightly. That pin looks like a weapon masquerading as clan allegiance. I'm forced to watch the hairs on his leg snag in the nap of my blue dress, combed through my skirt and left to connect us with annoying tendrils of clingy follicles. I wonder if they can inject sting if you misbehave the way a man-o-war jellyfish does with its long tentacles? He gives off that vibe. Disciplinarian, authoritarian, regent with an itchy trigger finger.

I tune back in to what he's saying, "...At the end of the car you will see the family tree. Everyone aboard the train this evening is here by exclusive invitation. You are the last remaining family of the esteemed Anton Dubois. He was an exceptionally wealthy man who left us a little mystery to solve. We know he amassed a fortune and even where he hid it, however we do not have the key to unlock the vault. He split the clues and evidence between the chosen descendants as his last act of superior defiance. One of you has the insight to reclaim the key. I got the train... and the combination. I have the map through the catacombs, and we have access to his private and clandestine railroads."

"Oh," I nod, never having heard of this ancestor.

"Think deeply, June. Where is the key?" urges McMorain, seduction thickening his tone.

"God!" I shrink back, pulling away from his foraging inquisition as if he reads minds. "I haven't the foggiest..."

"June," he murmurs, so imposing now I'm ungraciously cringing into the chair, "It's on board. We have deduced you will be the one to recall where Anton hid it."

"Why me? And then what?" I snap, bad mojo playing hopscotch across the vertebrae of my spine.

"You are here to solve mysteries, my dear. Anton takes as much as he gives. He'll make you earn this little reward." Leaving no room for personal privacy he says in my ear in a cloistered whisper, "But the reward is so worth it."

"But he's dead!" I snap, now pretty certain everyone here is pulling my leg just to see if I panic under duress. I glance for the hidden cameras again; I loathe reality telly with good reason.

Black nods, bumping elbows with me again, "He might be dead, but the paranormal is such a vague science with so many avenues which defy explanation that no possibility should be ruled out."

Plucking a cracker smothered in creamy fromage I cram it into my mouth just to buy time to think, endlessly playing elbow rock-paper-scissors with Black, and I'm clearly losing.

McMorain's hair in the velvet of my dress catches my focus again while I chew away in introspection, it bothers me enough that I feel like it's a curio for a collector of hair samples... samples that will be used in an intricate spell to cause a multitude of suffering.

"I'm always available if you need to talk," he says, patting my knee once more before retracting the indecent hand.

The dodgy git with the wheezing breath walks across the car to point a finger at me, "I've got it. You look like my grandmother."

Is that a compliment? I do not smell like lavender or use a gentian violet rinse, so no Mr Leery I do not look like your grandmother. She must be at least a hundred and forty by now.

McMorain smirks as if I spoke aloud which gives me a momentary pause of panic, but Black saves my bacon again, "You don't have a clue to the key, Henri. Unfortunately for you you're boarding the companion train to go home, so kindly abstain from harassing Miss Dubois."

Leery's left eye twitches and anger slips into his expression, "This isn't right. What about the rest of the heirs?"

"What about them?" drawls McMorain. "If you were significant Anton would have provided for you. Unfortunately for you he never forgets a slight, if you weren't gifted with a Dubois bestowed secret then he intended it to be that way. Consider it a deliberate omission and bow out with your dignity, man. We do not carry dead wood on board this Express."

No, you burn it to keep the locomotive running. That whistle sounds so very hungry for the souls of those with a vendetta to square, seething resentment seems like the perfect fuel which never goes out. It just burns and burns and burns, hotter and hotter. Vengeance is loads more effective than fossil fuel.

The whistle bellows agreement to McMorain's statement and the unholy squeal of metal screeching on metal drives a stake through my tenuous calm.

The train slides to a shuddering slow halt with the whistle demanding full disclosure and immediate departure of the family rejects.

I'm a little freaked out when everyone but Black and myself have been given walking papers, the staff handing out luggage while the human cargo disembark off the train from the viewing pen.

Lanky, the jacket swimmer, is escorted by Minion, and I'm relieved that it looks like Minion is leaving permanently to cross tracks onto a twin train with lights now shining at us across the way. It feels like pirating under a blanket of midnight. It's partly thrilling yet definitely alarming too.

When Manic Molly is the last person ostracised from the observation car, worry starts a steady trickle of overwrought adrenaline and cortisol. I gather she's going to whip them all into shape and make sure they toe the line, no questions asked. There was probably fine print on our invitations that can only be seen by the light of a black candle at full moon.

When Black and myself are the only two passengers left in the car it occurs to me that we're outnumbered by the eclectic people running this show.

Black offers me his bothersome elbow again and this time I take it out of the desire for comfort and need to be coupled close to an ally. The 'wrong' feeling has ratcheted up to engulf my every thought with wild scenarios, and I'm easily corralled to inspect the family tree.

Smiling at me, he points out my name, and then his.

We're miles apart, far distant cousins with nothing in common but a chromosome and surname.

"What's up, Crumpet? It's not like you to be so docile."

Shrugging, I glance behind us at the cabin crew. McMorain's taciturn stare has so much weight I feel manacled by it.

When I look back at the elaborate picture, Black pats my hand companionably where it rests in the crook of his arm.

"Did you know that almost ninety percent of humans are attracted to people who share common physical traits? A number of studies prove that us humans like to mate with people who look like us, perchance a way to perpetuate a strong DNA code, or signature bone structure and colouring," converses Black.

Disengaging myself from his elbow to put urgent distance between us, I'm examining him and his tone, trying to gauge if he's suggesting what I think he's suggesting.

Heat displaces the cold tentacle in my nape when McMorain hooks his hand on the back of my neck, locking me in his grip, framing me between the two gentlemen. His grip is dominant, threatening, forcing my stomach to cinch up to my throat in immediate apprehension.

"Good point Martin, that's very true. And it's been going on since time immemorial. Even intelligence may be a reason for matching genes in deliberate continuation. The royals did it for millennia, across the board," says McMorain conversationally, their tones belying the building undercurrent.

We're related, of course we look alike. So?

The train lurches when the brakes are released and the scything of metal against metal shrieks damnation at us.

On my designer stilts while my legs are snared in a narrow sleeve of skirt, I'm pitched forward toward the family tree displayed proudly in a gilt frame. Two pairs of hands halt my unstable trajectory toward the precious heirloom.

Planting my balance firmly underneath me again, I expect to be released, but they don't let go, they're glaring at each other over my head.... interminably.... and I'm too afraid to intervene in their visual conflict because it feels murderous.

"Captain, it's time to serve whisky," interjects a wavering voice as dry as the bones of its speaker.

Something creaks in the ceiling, helping to shatter the psychic duel. Dickens shuffles forward, watching my companions in such pale fear that he's tombstone grey. Proffering a tray of liquid pyre to McMorain, the tension locked on my person eases and I'm released from the biting fingers of my companions.

Black smirks as if victory was obtained in that silent clash.

"What will you be having?" asks the Captain, glancing at me with his smile implying 'I'm trying to be charming, follow my lead'.

I shake my head, just needing to get the heck away from the freak show. "Bed for me." Nodding at Black, then McMorain, I mutter, "Goodnight."

Turning away, I am tempted to run with haste as I hurry back to my room.

What the hell was all of that?

Give me a bloody break.

"So is this from the moonshine harvest?" I hear Black ask McMorain.

"The harvest has only just begun, the shadows are on the hunt," mumbles an answer as I vanish into the stately corridor.

Chapter 5

With plenty of privacy to get ready for bed and check my suite without any interruptions or impending responsibilities, I start at the door and run my hand over every surface. Finding no switch or latch or hidden lens, I then double check the lights, the closet, and behind the mirrors.

Nothing.

It's official, I'm paranoid... but I just can't shake the feeling I'm being watched.

Molly's gone off, along with a whole bunch of other people. I assume there are less than ten of us on board this train now, which means they surely have their hands full and won't be able to play Peeping Tom with the peculiar girl with the long black hair... and yet it still haunts me as surely as a pop up window saying '*I can see you*' when you've forgotten to switch off the camera after skyping with your bestie while she honeymoons in Spain.

I was mortified to think of how long they let me leave it on before saying anything. I'm allergic to modest clothing in the sanctuary of my own home and never wear a bra unless it's of vital import to world peace.

Whatever.

I *am* alone now, of this there is no doubt. The creepy feeling must be due to being in the weirdest situation of my life, on board a midnight train with trimmings and decorations so old they hiss latent antique energy into the atmosphere. Heck, if I'm sensitive to magnetic fields it's quite possible I can detect the lingering intent of the previous owners of these ancient items, or prior passengers.

It would explain the supernatural shadows and inexplicable breezes. Worried I'm heading for the loony bin, I choose the mental high ground. I am fierce, I am brave, I've got this... I am woman and I will not be running screaming for help again. If a spider crosses my path I will impale it with my ice-pick heels and Vlad it to the outside of my door for housekeeping to find.

I'm not a baby, or a feeble and flighty female in need of rescue and a cruddy elbow, and it's time I asserted myself in this unstable dynamic.

Moving to the bathroom I brush my teeth, use the loo, and open the cupboard to get my hairbrush. Standing in my daze I brush out my long hair, mulling mysteries and strange expectations.

Find the key... as if it's as easy as remembering. Yeah sure thing Rob Roy, I'll just get out my crystal ball and visit my ancestors past lives and hand over something you clearly shouldn't have access to. I'll give you the key and you'll feed me to the boiler so I can also wail inside the whistle, playing for the piper, forever steaming into the ether for angels to save me from your pit of eternal fire.

Ready to put the brush back, my spirit hiccups in and out of my body at the closed cupboard door.

Did I do that?

Blinking rapidly, I look around, sniffing for alien scents. I can always smell a stranger, but then here every smell is cryptic.

Shrugging it off, I open the cupboard and replace my brush, doing a quick glide of lip balm over my lips and a fast spritz of perfume to hide the smell of foreign linen when I'm in bed.

Why do they want us to think this coach is the Royal Scotsman? Is this a masquerade? A charade? A disguise? Is it this way because they know it won't get stopped and questioned?

The cupboard door is shut when I move to close it and my sixth sense grinds into apocalypse gear, levitating my soul out of my body to do the spirit quest three-sixty surveillance check.

Spinning around I check the bath, the panels, even looking up to see if Spider-man is dangling above me. A momentary darkness glances behind me in my periphery and I bolt straight to the bedroom, unzipping and sitting down, trying to calm the rapid fire of my escalated heartbeat.

I need mace, or... salt.

When nothing happens for a long while I dare to relax, thinking again of this masquerading train.

It's a great mask to transport fugitives... in fact the more I consider this 'cover', the more scheming and genius I think Anton Dubois was.

Colette...

A slither of ice runs down my cheek... my overactive imagination conjuring names into my ear. The weak light from the bedside lamp turns treacle dim, my skin crawling with the spooky catalyst. The hair over my shoulder moves aside as if I'm standing in front of a fan shaving dry ice into the room.

What would I have been without you? Already you doubt, question,... because you remember who truly owns the treasure.

Diving off the double bed, my dress loose, I step out of it and do the elbow arc of imminent cobweb attack now that my legs are free. It looks like samurai sword practice, which only makes it seem more like I know what I'm doing and can kick ass if need be. Whipping left, right, spinning and sparring to face all directions... I wonder if they put hallucinogens in the wine... or dinner? Or the cheese? Or in the air conditioning?

I'm not usually this prone to supernatural superstition.

This is mental!

I've brought the only satin slip I own to wear to bed. It reaches mid-thigh and is a deceptive little item because it has slinky spaghetti straps, yet it's warm and insulating. The kind of slip you end up wishing you could just slumber naked after sleeping in it for two hours.

I can't set my alarm clock because it won't work, and there is no alarm on the pocket watch. Am I to assume the whistle will wake us as if we're on the military express?

Yanking the black satin over my head, my focus skewers the item. The pocket watch.

Who did it belong to?

Instinctively picking it up I heft it in my palm, closing my eyes to 'sense' energy, tingles, hair prickles… anything.

That derisive low level laughter breathes across the tiny space again and I open my eyes, wondering if Black would be able to hear me if I spoke to empty air?

That would certainly solidify any preconceived notions he has of me being a walking fruit bat.

Something touches the space between my shoulder blades, caressing over my shoulder, freaking me the hell out. Wriggling uncontrollably in creep-induced spasms, I spin doing the 'one arm in sleeve-one arm out' styled cripple distortion, looking, knowing I'll find nothing. I'm alone. This is the wine messing with me.

I'm just oversensitive and reading into everything because I'm out of my comfort zone.

Yes, that must be it.

Wish I could have a cup of tea and a good book. I'll never sleep this hyped up on hair-raising séance-sense.

Climbing into bed, I stare up after killing the light, looking out the window as clouds weep long scuds across the leagues of sky at alarming speed. They look like waves on a midnight ocean twinkling stars as if moonlight is glistening off poachers nets bobbing on the occultation of high tide.

I thought we stopped at night? I guess that won't be happening now that the big reveal has happened. We all share blood, gathered tightly onto a main vein to travel to an undisclosed destination, the speed of the wheels causing the kind of friction that generates enough electricity to open wormholes and X portals.

History pervades the atmosphere with a weighty mantle of intrigue. What's the significance of us being related? McMorain and Black certainly don't seem to care for propriety. God above, am I related to Dickens? He gives me the total heebies.

Snuggling deeper under fabrics both silky smooth and duck-down heavy, I sag into the deceptive comfort of luxury. I watch the sky whizz past the isolated window, unperturbed. No one can sneak a quick spy in this pane. One plus for the travelling casket.

Pain for windows, a smoker at the helm, a wailing whistle exhaling in conversation, the cursing piper, and secrets. Quite a cocktail.

I'm already dozing when insistent breath hisses in my ear, tickling the hairs, *Colette*.

"Mmmm," I object, rolling away and covering my ear with my arm.

A strong grip spikes my neck to the bed and this time I'm awake and alarmed, thrashing and struggling against the aggression pinning me.

The moon's rays boldly display that there is no one above me, but I know there is! I can *feel* it. Shivers ride my skin into slithering taut objection; forewarning malicious motivations.

He's strong, and heavy. Breath baptises my eyelashes and a disgusting sensation licks down my cheek, onto my lips, leaking sin in a slimy trail to my throat.

My heart detonates, banging epileptically in my chest 'til it hurts, my ability to breathe impaired and laboured. Blinking in disbelief, I wriggle and buck, fighting for air when my veins begin to throb across my temples from constriction. It feels just like a hand throttling when I'm given a silent warning of strangulation.

An invisible finger presses onto my lips, my arm thrust away from my ear and the pillow depressed with the capturing force as if someone just pinioned me, *Colette, shhh, it's me, papa.*

Who? What? This isn't happening. It's your imagination, June. Just count to ten and everything will be fine.

My hair bunches as if threaded around a fist, my scalp objecting in searing agony. I wince, squealing in high pitched terror, forcing myself to open my eyes to assure myself this is just a dream, it's not real.

When a hand starts thumbing my nipple like a priest fixating on a rosary, I flip. "**Heeel**....!" I wheeze, instantly regretting it when a knee bangs hard into the gap between my legs, debilitating me.

Shhh! Colette, what did I say about screaming? If you scream the others will die. Don't try my patience on this.

Panting with panic, my ears blocking from fear, I lie still, trying to think my way out of this. My throat works in dry upheaval, adrenaline injecting liquid nitrogen down my spine, dizziness hooding my focus with paralysing terror.

Density squashes me, so cold and heavy I feel buried alive, the grip on my hair holding me fast, the knee still between my legs so hard and invasive even my tendons hurt. Pain keeps knifing up to my stomach and I'm having a fucking hard time believing this is a dream. It's visceral. This is bloody happening!

Oh god.....

Will the lord's prayer work?

I don't wear a cross and I'm not in the habit of walking around with a conveniently placed vial of holy water either.

His voice speaks again, this time as if regretting his previous tone, and I'm wondering if it's telepathic, *You know I love you. It's right. No one loves you like I do. No one will take care of you the way I do.*

Helpless tears gather and drip when the paranormal visitation slides my slip up with a coarse hand, tracing my thigh and then my stomach; it flicks back the linen covering me and arctic air traverses over my skin in spectral trails of delicate affection.

Oh god, oh god! Please!

My panic catapults and quadruples when another set of hands cup my boobs to squeeze them like stress balls.

I try to scream but petrified terror laces my vocal chords with silence serum. All I'm wailing are exaggerated exhalations.

It's mortifying and humiliating to be held down by nothing, wrestling pointlessly with the thin air manhandling me.

Rolled, my strength is moot, I can't move. I don't know if this is fear induced paralysis, mental denial, or truly a case of being bullied by ghosts more real than poltergeists, but I'm captured between solid forms, unable to do anything more than whimper. My insides quiver with harsh ripples, focus scattering in numb horror.

Tears mingle with foreign breath, my leg shoved into the air like a deformed ballerina and the acute sensation of forced penetration rams into me.

I'm dry, it pulls, churning incinerating fire up both my legs while my heart goes into hiding, feeling like it's being chopped in a juicer. Jolted up with the next thrust, I'm pounded by an entity who is a right fucking maniac. It hurts, the agony now cremating all sensation but the harsh hold on my neck exerted from behind, the diabolical breath chuckling in my ear by co-pilot, his rigid excitement busy finger painting my backside as if he's contemplating joining this depraved ménage à trois.

It's mental terror experiencing enforced intercourse when you can't fight it.

The train rocks with mocking motion, smacking my head into the mahogany panelling, turning my disgracing violation into the ambient sound of a train's rhythm.

Bang... bang... thump thump... grunt grunt... rasp...

I'm whimpering, choking, crying hysterically, unable to find the strength to scream while demolishing thrusts stake inside me with the excruciating disfigurement of a brand.

Cauterising my body, it punches unnaturally, without glide, yanking my insides in rough snagging, it chafes enough to leave blisters and I just want it to stop.

Exhalations ensue, heavy breathing washing my face in alcoholic breath, all while I stare up at the world blurring past. Upside down, I want to half believe I'm on a fun ride in a scary theme park. This is just a special effect. It's not real.

Fingers bite into my cheeks and the spectre assumes a shadow, glaring down at me with the visage of Mr Black, *I am real.*

Yanked and violently flipped, I'm suffocating on pedigree swan down neatly sewn in precise squares while the outcast from the past has his ethereal way with me. His head leaves a crater in the pillow, his eyes staring into me to witness my shame. His ego needing the boost of seeing me cry, listening to me fight for air with the acute fascination of a stethoscope, taking smug satisfaction in his supremacy.

Smothering in an endless cloak of cold, nausea pickles my insides with the sensitivity of formaldehyde when I observe his grimace of gratuity. The madness is there in his eyes, the anger mingled with lunacy, capricious and accustomed to getting his own way, even by force.

My fingers are numb from inflicted pressure, my lungs so tight I'm struggling to inhale, my hip bone biting into something beneath me, like a belt buckle.

I'm left bruised and battered by his archaic technique.

The ghost train has a resident rapist and I'm the only female on board that I'm aware of. No wonder Molly is such a Grade A bitch.

My degradation is swallowed by a bilious wave when the other entity takes a turn, his thrust such a hard punch it feels like he just ruptured right through my uterus. Shoved closer to Black's weird ghost clone, despising his satisfied smile, I'm brutally ridden as if the geist is in a camel race. It's endless, fast, fragmenting the room as my vision is shunted by enthusiasm.

My legs shake, my voice shudders in heavy gasps as he fucks the air out of me in an endless parody of ecstasy. Imaginary balls flog my thighs with inertia, legs inside my own forcing mine so unnaturally my bones protest.

Squashed into the pillow, I'm held off the bed by my hips, my spine compacting with each and every ruthless dowsing of the devil's penis. It's gone on for so long wet heat is trickling down my thigh, my sinuses clogging from snivelling, and I know I've gone mad.

Entity number one looks fondly at me as if I'm doing god's duty here, reaching across the double bed to stroke my face while his co-pilot widens my body in the arrival of his despicable phantgasm.

Colette, look at them, they are pure, they're ours, you make me so proud.

Fuck!

Ignited with fight I scramble, flay, grapple, struggle, and find my scream. This time I do such an impressive soprano shriek the spectres look like they're being electrocuted, shrinking up to the ceiling and giving me room to run... and flee I do.

Stumbling over my own feet, slamming my hip into the corner of the dressing table, I reach the door, unlock it, fling it wide, screeching wild lightning into the sleeping silence only to have a savage grip in my hair bodily lift me and hurl me into the veneered wall less than two meters behind me.

Crawling forwards, spidering over the infected carpet saturated in aeons of history, I keep screaming through the tears, desperation engulfing every sense but self-preservation.

"June?" I discern in the cosmic stealth beyond the door.

"Heeel..p.!"

This time blood explodes in my mouth and phantom Black materialises in front of me, his fist pulled back for round two when I huddle with my arms over my head to frantically shriek.

The room is glacial, too dark to be natural, and thick with the scent of blood and sweat.

Blows rain onto my forearms until they throb, my sobbing now the only focus I have to keep my heart beating, hiding my sanity in a little pocket of dark anguish where he can't reach it.

Colette! **Colette!**

When hard arms clamp around me I lose it and start thrashing in the last stand of a desperate woman.

"Woah, it's me. Calm down, Crumpet. Where's the light switch?"

As if on cue the overhead light flicks on and as Black releases me to stand I spy two faces peering curiously at me from the open door.

Dickens is dressed like Wee Willie Winkie and McMorain is in nothing more than black boxers.

"What's going on here?" demands the Captain.

Black faces the interrogation, explaining, "It sounded like she was being attacked."

"I was..." I whisper tremulously. Relief mingles a potent hybrid with hysteria and my sobs magnify.

I'm okay. He's gone. I'm okay. Calm down.

Suddenly self-conscious, I attempt a stand to pull my short slip down for modesty, but my legs give when I see the dark rivulets snaking down the inside of my thighs to my knees, pooling in every crevice. Instantly weak I'm forced to haul myself up using the chair placed opposite the door.

Black turns back to me, helping me into the chair, lifting my chin to swivel my face for his inspection.

"Bruised legs, bloody face, scratches and swelling on arms... if this is delusional self-abuse she's a rare case." Tilting my head further he looks into my eyes after scanning my neck, whispering, "Are you into auto-erotic asphyxiation? Is this why you wore that scarf? Those are impressive bruises, June."

I shake my head, giving him a reproachful stare.

"Shut up, Martin," snaps McMorain, walking into my suite to sit on my bed, watching me as if I am a curiosity they found at the bottom of a purple lake in darkest Africa. "June, why don't you tell us what happened?"

"Gh-ost..." Keening uncontrollably, I stare my distress at the ceiling. I can't tell three men I was raped by a freaking phantom. I'll be in the fitted jacket with buckles and long sleeves before the next station. Going for the logical approach, biting on my lip to stop the quivering of my chin, I inhale dramatically and mutter over a split lip, "He kept calling me Colette."

This gets everyone's attention and again I feel like experiment A while all the others who left were the placebo group who got to escape early.

"What?" I demand.

Their reaction was the sanity I needed. It's a slice of redemption before the core of me unravels in shock.

Black offers me his effing elbow, "Come with me."

I just got shagged within an inch of my life. My lady bits are throbbing with every beat of my heart and feel swollen to the size of your testicles, if you think I can walk normally now, you would be wrong.

Men are ignorant idiots at the best of times.

McMorain has this weird ESP knack because he shakes his head, "Leave her, Martin. She doesn't need to see the family tree, we can explain it to her right here."

They share one of those looks that lets everyone else know they're communicating without saying a word.

Pulling the bureaucratic strings McMorain looks at Dickens, "Kindly get Miss Dubois a strong drink."

"A normal one," I mutter. "Like a Cosmo, or just a martini... something normal."

Black gives me his 'I just struck gold' smile. "Martini? Subconscious preferences or what, eh Crumpet?"

Ignoring Black's conversation, McMorain starts talking as soon as Dickens shuffles off, "He loved Colette best, her name is significant."

"Who's *he*?" I ask, already confused.

"Anton Dubois. The family starts with Anton and Mari. Mari died after having a child, a girl. Without an heir to carry the family name, well it was a problem for Anton, one he set out to rectify without going on the pull. No courtship required."

I nod, telling them, "I think lightning struck the family tree. He told me he was papa, and he... uhm... *splutter*."

The Captain nods, giving me a surprisingly understanding smile, "I know. Incest. He loved Colette best because she gave him a son, and kept on popping them out until he had enough offspring to begin this empire."

Oh god above! We're descendants of incest? Isn't that like... **bad?** That could cause restless spirits, surely?

Black sits down on the dressing table and says to McMorain, "Why Colette? Aside from the obvious of course."

I get the impression he said that for my benefit. My thighs are pulsating, my vagina is singeing, and my nipples feel like I was swung around by them. Edgy, I fidget with the hem of my slip, wishing I could bath, and get a hug, and a sedative, and a burning stake, and a gun loaded with silver bullets.

"Cole – the shortened version of her name and the male aspect of it – means black. Colette means 'victory of the people'. This was Dubois' sense of humour at its finest. A black heart is a victorious one – over many, and his firstborn is the conqueror, even his," explains McMorain.

Glancing at Martin Dubois, it bothers me instantly that I called him Black out of pure instinct.

He stares back at me as if hearing my thoughts loud and clear.

An austere pall dulls the atmosphere of the suite and McMorain stands, looking down at me as the tension stretches.

"What did he look like?"

It's the true test. Don't you need a stick before you start poking the vulnerable? Morbid curiosity has no finesse or compassion.

Here goes nothing. "Mostly like you," I say to Martin.

I'm not going to call him Black ever again.

Looking back at the Captain, I add, "But you look a lot like Martin, just older."

He looks to Martin, saying, "I knew it. We've come back, we're multiplying, and they needed to know their mate before letting us have her. They've anchored." Then he turns, staring down at me with the darkness of Satan's grimoire, "And you are the spitting image of Colette."

That leaves me speechless and alarmed.

What?

"You totally qualify. You're unmarried, you have the family name, and you look like her. We knew if anyone would stir Anton out of his occult coma, it would be you," says Martin. "You're the key we were looking for. You unlocked the vault of our souls just by being on board. With you here we can finally continue our legacy without boundaries."

My leg starts twitching uncontrollably and I press the heel of my palm on my knee to halt the bounce, "You set me up? This is a trap?"

Martin smiles, shaking his head, standing, covering the gap in one stride, "I *am* Anton."

McMorain joins his doppelganger, "And I am also Anton Martin Dubois."

"And you are our key," smiles Martin, with the manic grin of the man who just hurt me.

McMorain leans over my chair, a hand on either arm, forcing me into retreat against the unforgiving back of it, "I want a new son, Colette. You gave yourself to my soul before you gave yourself to me. Why do you insist on always defying the only man to own you?"

"The other family members were weak. Only good for recycling," says Dickens from the doorway. "You are not weak, but still as difficult as ever, madam."

He parts my jailers to offer me a tall glass of red stuff. "It's a Bloody Mary. It seemed apt considering Mari died giving birth to you." Then he looks at the blood congealing on my chair, giving it significance. "The blood covenant, you already give life to the masters brothers."

"This isn't happening." I shake my head, covering my ears, hoping it's just a dream.

I went to bed and I'm having nightmares.

Wake up, June. Wake up!

"You were born in June," explains Mephisto McMorain.

"This is sick! You're saying you're my *father* and... I **won't!**"

"There's no escape from this train," smiles Martin, his expression ever more sinister and menacing. "Look outside, haven't you noticed it has been night for too long? The sun doesn't shine where we are."

"How do you live with yourself?" I demand, staring at both manifestations.

I don't understand how this is possible but Black hinted at the mystery over cheese and wine. One of me, two of them, and how many more? Do they murder their children to forge a new Anton? They want more infants, to breed? So that they have innocent lives to offer in exchange for their rituals?

Never eat cheese before bed. Everyone knows that.

Now I understand why they kept pushing me to be with Black. The others weren't sent home, they're filling larders and furnaces – 'recycled'. The train is wailing. It's suffering.

I was the only one reserved, kept on board to continue the journey. And they are clearly madder than inbred hicks.

Arcane breath breathes in my face when McMorain bends over me again, gripping my throat as if I've been his submissive for years, "My turn. Then his," he nudges his head toward Black.

I'm in hell. This is bullshit! I'll die before this nocturnal nightmare is over. Who the hell do these psychopaths think they are? I'm June, not Colette. I'm sane, the only one in the travelling asylum. Fear at the expression in his eyes vices my veins, his smile sharper than the athame used to harvest hearts, my spirit thrust into instant famine by my future aboard this aberration.

When he releases me I struggle to stand, but do, with disfigured dignity, looking at them one by one, "I want to see the family tree."

And being the gullible sods they are, they let the lady go first. They think I'm off to satisfy my curiosity.

I take a shaky stroll all the way to the observation car, cupping my slip between my legs, afraid to even look at the ruptures and bruising, biding my time and gauging my reserves, relieved to see the door to the viewing deck still open...

It's all or nothing. Them or me. Pain now rather than eternally.

... I **run**.

Sprinting for the balustrade with cramping muscles, extravasation destroying living tissue deep within, I dive over the wooden barrier, choosing death over bondage, free-falling into the dark... and there is no railroad, no metal track, nothing but endless void.

I braced myself for stone, impact, pain, wind... and it's all missing.

Men yell, hands reach out, but they're too slow.

"I own your soul, Colette! You can run but you will never escape! I gave you life and I owned it before you were born! I will always own it!"

The last thing I hear before losing oxygen is the grief stricken lament of a train's whistle screaming mutiny into purgatory.

It's endless, spinning around and around me in generations of torment, binding me inside the cocoon of scarlet steam and a highland knell. Acutely aware of the dearth in my veins I close my eyes to welcome death and hope, wishing there was shine to be found in moonshine.

Clear as diamonds but murkier than mud, it's a lethal potion to justify Anton's insane tyranny.

It's devil's juice which they blend with sangre-wine. Anton's familial sangria. His addictive contraband. If you make enough deals you can split up your soul and coexist with yourself, hunting the one who escaped, maintaining life by consuming the slain kin. They'll die without me, I realise in hindsight. Well good! Seal that crypt of depraved hedonism.

I've escaped the Moonshine Express!

Twice.

Why do I never remember when I resurface? Why do I date Martin knowing he's going to hurt me? He's named after the god of war, his colour is *red*, and yet I stupidly fall under his spell and end up in his bed. The clues were all there and yet I recognised none.

I own you! taunts through nebulous necrosis.

My father, my enemy, my family who thrive on lies instead of love... I must not wake this time. Let it end.

It *must* end.

A soft strain ribbons across the chasm of endless ink. It calls to me, plucking the notes in my heart, healing, beckoning.

I must follow it. I can't resist. A kilted warrior plays the pipes so I can find my way to whole, fishing me back on a hook snagged deep in my soul.

It's a sorcerous cord connected to my forever, reeling me in. The closer I get to the panacea, the mundane things unravel. My name, my address, amnesia mummifies me. I'm the mother who never weds, destined to lie in daddy's bed.

Opening my eyes I look at my lover while a train blows off hot steam in the distance. I dreamt of a train... I think? He rolls, prying open one eye, his hair a mess.

"You had one of those dreams again. Nicolette you shouldn't drink before bed, you know that."

Er. Who are you again?

Automatically looking for wedding rings, I assume it's just a brief fray into carnal captivity.

He arches two disapproving black eyebrows. "Don't tell me, you forgot my name again?"

Utterly embarrassed, I nod.

He sits up and starts tickling me under the duvet until I'm squealing for mercy. "Martin. For the last time woman my name is Martin! And in case you forgot, we are booked on that trip today, so tick-tock Crumpet, we're going to be late if you don't get your sexy little arse out of bed."

I know I had a bad dream which has left an acrimonious stain on my soul, instilling unease. If it was a premonition, or past life memory, I'll never know because my head is pounding and I need to find the Aspirin.

"Come on Nicki..." he orders, offering me his hand. Staring at the scratches all over him I wonder just how wild it got last night. "And you're going to have to wear your scarf, to hide... er... your vice." He motions across his neck.

His wink seals a fate and I have that wee niggly feeling doing the Highland Fling in my gut.

Pulled out of bed, spying the invitations to journey on an exclusive train waiting patiently on the bedside table, I have the impression we're off for the ride of our lives.

This is his logic. I have a pathological fear of trains. Despite all the holes in my memory, I know that much.

M...*artin* (?) insists the only way to overcome a fear is to face it.

How bad can it be? It's just an innocuous train, the trip is only three days.

The peanut gallery in the back of my head pipes up, *it's always three days in the underworld, always.*

You need church girl, not dinner for three into eternity.

He presses his iPod to play through the speakers and the second the strains of highland bagpipes flit into the room my doubt diffuses.

It's soporific, lulling me into a haven of safety. I'm overreacting again, as usual.

"You're going to love it babes, the Captain wears a kilt. You'll be in your element. You were born for an environment like that, you'll feel like you've come home when you step aboard."

He's right of course. Nodding with sedation, I smile reassurance, "I'm sure I'll love it."

"And he'll love you," winks Martin. "He'll want to abduct you to his den and have lots of babies with you."

"Now you're just blowing it out your arse darling. I doubt the sun shines out his."

"Moonshine maybe," he laughs, pulling me with his arm around my shoulders toward the shower.

I hobble, feeling a tad tender.

"I must be moving up in the world," I smirk, disguising my objecting body with idle chatter, picking up my toothbrush.

"Or going down on it," he volleys, flicking my leg with his already wet facecloth.

In the distilled light of day, I think Martin's right. We need an adventure, and this one is elite, by invitation only. Staring at the bourbon sky beyond the open shutters, I vow to never drink again, or eat cheese before bed.

~End of Part 1~

Part II

Crystal Fire

Chapter 1

You'd think the steam from the shower filled the world because when I open the front door the beautiful sunny day is gone and in its place is a dull vacuum where sound refuses to travel.

*

Mist so low it qualifies as fog holds the planet hostage in a thick veil of anthrax gas, concealing everything but the next meter of road. Crawling along in the taxi I almost celebrate when we stop at the station to board the train.

Martin holds my hand in a firm grip, the kind of vice-hold used on a small child who is irritable and petulant and about to throw a tantrum. I know this trip is important to him and I'm going to force myself onto this mobile death-trap if it kills me.

Pulled by his hand harness along the wet platform, anxiety smears my perspective with foreboding.

Out of the unholy soup I spy red, the melody of a soul in writhing pain melting my hesitance and sucking me closer in sacred appreciation.

We hurry around a Drum Major playing pipes with the ease of a piccolo. Nodding as we pass him, his expression is jovial, and oddly he reminds me of Martin.

"That could be you in a few years," I smile at my companion.

"Wishful thinking, Crumpet?" he winks at me, clearly declining the suggestion.

Reaching the end of a royal carpet, the two waiting in ambush nearly give me cardiac arrest. Standing in the entrance to the train is a woman shorter than me with spiky black hair, in the grips of snogging a coffin dodger.

Ugh, that's just sick.

Martin clears his throat impatiently and the two lovebirds split as cleanly as lightning striking wood. Air pockets expand and explode the two asunder when the loco adds to Martin's impolite announcement, filling the fog with a warbled wail.

Tweedledee with her short hair gives us a tepid smile of welcome while Tweedledum offers a nerve-splicing homicidal smile.

The Highland Fling is morphing into Spicy McHaggis and I'm doubting my sanity at even entertaining the thought of stepping into the confines with those two.

Martin shoves the invitations in her face and she gives him a lascivious smirk, licking her lips while giving him the once over.

Do that again and I'll show you it is possible to tie a knot in a tongue.

"Mr Dubois, we are delighted to welcome you onto our esteemed chariot," she gushes.

Next thing she'll be sliding up and down a stripper's pole to show him how very juicy she is.

Give me a fucking break.

Tweedledum nods at me and I wonder if he's been fumigated lately. Good lord, she was kissing mausoleum breath? Eeek.

Martin, don't you let that mouth near your dick or I'm never touching it again. It'll rot and fall off quickstix.

Shuddering, I'm grateful to have my manly shield to hide behind as he leads us to our suite. Looking beyond him, the intricate door marked as Personnel Only intrigues me.

This is reminiscent of a treasure hunt. It's like being aboard the Orient Express playing a form of Cluedo. I'm itching to go investigating.

Diving onto the double bed, he folds his hands behind his head to stare at the ornate décor, "I hate boarding late. We missed dinner and everything. Now we're expected to just go to bed and start the fun in the morning."

I would suggest starting the fun now but I'm not entirely positive my body can withstand whatever we did last night two nights running.

I feel like I've been training for Olympic gymnastics.

And how did I just magically lose hours? Last I checked it was afternoon.

"Isn't there like a drink's car, or something?" I suggest.

He hinges upright, shrugging off his jacket, "Yes! Let's flatten a bottle of bubbly, then we can come back here and christen this bed."

Let's make that three bottles of bubbly and good luck to mini-Martin in his bid to resurrect his libido after that.

Nodding, leaving my coat next to his, I put my arm through Martin's as we go off to investigate the exquisite temple of mobile history.

Entering the lounge car, I'm taken aback to see the dude with the kilt sitting chatting to the circus escapees.

Tweedledee points to a bucket of ice with gold necks peeking out of it, "Help yourself to champers. Sorry for the weak reception but it's been a torrid few days."

Martin just abandons me in his haste to get legless, and I'm left feeling like I've turned into a fishing sinker by the sordid stare of the man who looks like an older version of him.

He pats the seat next to him, "I don't bite."

I'm not buying it. I think he does bite, the kind that leaves hickeys for a century.

"Don't be rude, Crumpet," whispers in my ear.

Glancing up at Martin, I give him the silent beseeching plea for help, but he's already looking forward to seeing how loudly he can make that cork canon. The tearing of foil rifles through the expectant silence and I watch Martin's back, knowing I'm forgotten and dismissed.

Will he ever grow up? I swear that boy really wanted to be in the Crimean war. Maybe he should join a re-enactment club or something, and work it out of his system.

Looking back at Red Plaid, the man in the skirt is still waiting. Inhaling a waft of courage I force my legs to move in his direction, sinking stiffly onto the padded spot vacantly waiting for my arse.

"What's your name?" he says conversationally.

Meeting his curious stare, I mumble, "Nicki."

"Nicolette. Her name is Nicolette," corrects Martin. "And I am Martin Dubois."

Martin crosses the gap to quickly shake hands in the gentleman's code, following the moment with a tympanic shattering POP.

"You can call me Captain," nods Red Plaid to Martin, then swivels his gaze back to me.

Black eyes simmer with unveiled desire and I get the sandy grit of distaste in my mouth.

Creep.

Martin plops down next to Shifty and she puts her hand on his thigh, indicating the bottle with the inclination of her head, "Pour us all a glass?"

Hellooooo? You're here to serve us, not the other way around pop tart!

And like a well-heeled darling, the idiot does! Passing out fizzy froth to all of us.

Great, I hate red champagne.

Taking mine politely, I give an insipid smile, watching that woman with my scimitar sharp stare.

Touch him again and I swear to god you'll never suck another lolly.

She smiles at me, raising her flute in a mocking toast. Sipping mine experimentally I almost spill the lot when a hand rests on my thigh.

Leaping up out of reflex, I stare at the heathen in shock.

He looks innocently at me and simply pats that fucking cushion again. Condescendingly saying silently, *Come on Crumpet, show us your tits. Come sit in Uncle Plaid's lap. I'll give you a sweetie.*

What the hell are you doing, man? I stare at Martin, but he seems completely unfazed by this bizarre behaviour.

Is this like a swinger's trip or something?

Martin, I am going to decapitate you! You set me up!

Fuuuuuhk.

Getting spine crawl, I announce, "I have a migraine. I'll see you all in the morning."

I don't wait for approval, I don't care if I'm rude, I'm getting the heck away from that party. Oh god! What if they expect me to fondle decomposing dickface?

Jesus!

Rushing down the passage, losing the lilt of voices and conversation, I find myself alone with that fascinating door at the end of the carriage. It's whispering somnolent temptation at me as surely as the magic looking glass.

Let me just get ready for bed, then I'll sneak behind there and nose about while they're distracted by their erotic indulgences, participating in the lounge car orgy.

Screw you, Martin. You are so not getting any tonight.

Chapter 2

Curiosity compels me to creep deeper down the gloomy passage, thickened with cobwebs of shadow clinging to corners and casting a sordid darkness down the length of the car.

I hear movement which piques the sleuth in me, sucking my feet to the ajar door as surely as iron to a magnet.

My pulse panics when I peer into the room which is dancing in agitated candlelight, distorting all surfaces under a diaphanous wave of undulations.

"Don't be shy mademoiselle. Come in," beckons a warm baritone beyond my view.

Carefully planting five tense fingers rigidly on carved ebony, I urge the door to widen on its hinges, silently expanding my observation into the crypt beyond.

A man stands with his back to me, wearing a blue velveteen smoking jacket with white lace cuffs protruding out of each sleeve to embalm his hands.

One of those hands is steadily above a candle, holding parchment which is catching flame, scorching it instantly to demise, saturating the room with the scent of cinders.

He cocks his head, speaking intimately as if sharing a cipher, "Hear that? The drums speak."

Fascinated with his historical attire and the long obsidian hair caught in the nape of his neck in a single twine of black leather, I watch the gloss capture and hold the light when he moves his head.

Knowing he can't see my surveillance I peruse the length of him, from the thigh hugging basalt breeches to the high sheen of his matching boots. His trousers suck to his backside as if sewn directly onto him and then dipped in molten bronze, shamelessly showing off musculature I haven't seen in... phwoar... ages.

He glances at me, the tether on his hair coming loose with the motion, framing onyx eyes in soft mystery, his smirk deceptively demure, "I'm glad you had the courage to come and find me."

Turning to fully face me he drops the burning page into a pewter dish to give me his full attention, and I'm shell-shocked.

He looks like Martin. Exactly identical! Well... except for the little fact that he's hotter, definitely stronger, his hair is longer and curling sensually over his collar in lazy swirls, his face has scruff on it giving him a rogue demeanour, and he's outstanding to gawk at.

This is just too weird for words.

"And what do you call yourself, mademoiselle?" he purrs, stepping closer so I'm forced to retreat, bumping a Victorian lady's chair, plopping ungracefully into it as I lose my balance.

"Nicki... er... Nicolette."

"Hmmm," he murmurs, rubbing his chin as if examining a peculiar specimen. Bowing slightly in a stiff manor, hand on chest, pupils glued on me like sniper beams, he says, "And of course I am Count Anton."

"C...ount?"

Abacus? Abraxus? What kind of count? Dracula kind? Accountant kind?

He makes me fidgety and I'm finding it hard to hold his gaze, glancing about, taking in everything at once like an ADD who forgot her Ritalin.

It's messy in here, full of old knickknacks and priceless trinkets. The walls are charcoal brocade, which is fucking awesome stuff, and I wonder if Laura Ashley will ever join this trend because I am so *in* if she is... and and and... good lord those are very red candles.

What was he burning?

"But you can call me Anton," he murmurs, capturing my hand and kissing the back of it, and it's a damn good thing I'm sitting down or I'd now be a paraplegic squashing his shiny boots.

"N...n nice to meet you..." Do I say your highness? What a daft thing to say because clearly I am sitting down and he is standing, and that's like stating the obvious... but decorum would dictate I defer respect... however my tongue is currently making cridhes and it's useless for anything but drooling and blowing heart shaped bubbles.

The chair I'm in is Guinness rich and just as sable, and I'm finding his hold on my hand is spiking my heartbeat as effectively as defibrillator paddles.

This is a lesson in chemistry with an alchemist, 101. I'm clearly the idiot here being suffered by a genius.

A nefarious smile aims at me, his eyes deep pools of esoteric temptation, and when he relinquishes my hand I'm tempted to pout.

"As I recall, you forgot to sign the waiver form on boarding did you not? Ni-koh-lette?"

The candles flare with the brilliance of rising phoenix's and the room melts into a pond of lust right along with me. I would live an eternity to hear the way he says my name. Fuckness, it could strip the corset off any frigid debutante.

I nod, just to stay in his company, hoping he'll drop my name again in that foreign lilt, as if he's making love and whispering it in my ear, full of praise and passion.

Grrrrrrrumptious.

He indicates the table where he was standing when I nosily snooped this far without a chaperone. "It's on the table, do you mind? It's so much easier to relax and enjoy fine company when business isn't lingering in the periphery."

To emphasise his metaphor he looks to the shrouded corners worming with excited shadows dancing the candle-shade frenzy.

"Oh. Right. Of course," I nod, as if I do this sort of thing *all* the time and am *so* familiar with the protocol.

Attempting to stand on legs under siege by the lethargic sap of desire, I balance carefully, experiencing a blizzard of incriminating warmth lazing in the hollow of my hips... pulsating wanton intrigue in endless bolts of stimulation.

Just breathe, don't trip and smack your head, and for Thor's sake make sure your hand doesn't shake.

He clasps my elbow, encouraging me with insistent strength to the magi's table covered in pitch cloth and scattered with treasures I'd love to examine if he wasn't standing right next to me, heating my arm with velvet sheathed muscles and intoxicating cologne.

Reaching the nook he retrieves a contract off the top of a pile and places it in front of me. It's a small page, hand written on ancient vellum, probably dating back to the inception of this train.

Standing with him, the world wavers as though I just stepped into a different realm, my lungs contracting as if the air is denser.

No Nicki, the only thing denser is you. Snap out of it.

He passes me the fountain pen waiting next to the inkwell, indicating I should have at it.

The writing is too small to read but the dotted line is clear as Cupid's arrow. I've never used a fountain pen before. It feels unnatural and heavy.

Spying my discomfort he folds his hand over mine, guiding it to the ink, "Dip it in here, gently,"... and we do, *together*, "And then give it a careful shake to disperse any droplets, this prevents blotting on the page..."

He snaps my hand in a jerky motion with the tip of the pen still in the glass lip of the jar, and it's so salacious and deeply suggestive that I'm blushing. Heat chases my cheeks while I think of how delightful it sounds to be an ink blotter under a fountaining pen.

I'm fixating on the neat fingernails and the bulge of muscle next to his thumb where he gloves my hand with blunt elegance. With his voice so close, the way he's holding me, I'm balanced somewhere between a child being tutored and a randy teenager needing a quickie before we're caught.

I have the illogical reflex to relax against him where he stands behind me... and just breathe him in. Of course that lovely charade will be followed with much humiliation and grovelling while I wheedle to get him to say my name again.

"Sign, Ni-koh-lette," he says, perverting my name in his masculine timbre. I can hear him smiling and twist to look up, desperate to witness it.

Oh Jesus, he's so near. If I lift onto my tiptoes I could kiss him. That's one diabolical smile... naughty, illicit, drenched in wicked promises of adoring sin. He's the kind of man you want to catch smiling... a lot.

I can make you smile, oh yes, just give me five minutes of your precious time...

What? What the hell Nicki, get with the program, asap!

Blinking as rapidly as my perplexed heartbeat, I nod, looking back at the waiting page splayed in sacrifice on the tabletop, and I bend, screwing up my eyes to see if I need to date it or something.

Ha, date it. I'd lurrrve to date him.

Martin will of course send me to 'how to train your submissive' school if I did, but I think I wouldn't rightly care. This is soul mate attraction I'm harbouring and it's eating me with aphrodisiac fire from the inside out. I am feverish, and my undies are definitely collecting incriminating evidence to accuse me as guilty of licentious thoughts over a complete stranger.

But he looks like Martin, and in court that's my defence. It was dark your honour. I love him your honour. Oh yes we always get violent your honour. I'd show you the bruises but only if you let him strip me, slowly, with his teeth.

I wonder how he tastes. Would he be opposed to biting?

Shit! I just nicked right through my lip and now the fucker is bleeding. Very attractive Nicki. He'll definitely want to kiss you now that you have blood seeping between your pearly whites.

Ugh, so gross.

Just sign.

Sign!

Sucking my lip, I use too much pressure to hide my trembling when I scribble my name on the dotted line, wondering why it had to be such an ordeal.

His hand obnoxiously glides over my glute just before I'm about to stand upright and offer his pen back, and I end up dropping it when my fingers go weak, in a loud clatter and dramatic scandalised inhalation.

A little lower and a little to the right and... Shut up Nicki!

Closing my eyes, gripping the edge of the table, I dig deep to resurrect societal conditioning and self-control. Taking a calming breath, hoping the dizziness subsides, I pray I look normal when I stand erect and give him a polite smile.

I must behave like a lady, not a nookie hunter out on the prowl. Women are robots expected to be good when all we really want to do is lick and taste and ride to Haydes.

With poise reinstated I don't know what to do now. What's the correct conduct, the 'thing' to say now that business has been concluded?

Proximity scatters my thoughts into useless kaleidoscopes when he lifts my chin, looking at my mouth. "You are bleeding."

Gee, thanks for stating the obvious.

"Uh, huh," I mumble, currently unable to nod, unwilling to breathe as he examines my mouth with the discerning attention to detail you'd expect from an ENT specialist.

"Does it hurt?"

"Nah uh," I try to shake my head but his grip prevents it.

Astral irises flick to stare into my own, his other hand oh so conveniently joined to his arm is snaking around my middle... and I don't think I'm going anywhere just yet. I might have a stroke though, if my pounding heart doesn't learn to apply zenitation.

"May I..." he murmurs, hot exhalations skating over my lips, breathing into the mouth he's holding open rather effectively.

May you what? This is like going to the dentist and trying to hold a conversation while condom smelling fingers are shoved in your gob.

"...Kiss it better?"

Oh sweet lollies. Yes!

"Uh, huh," I breathe, my legs getting that 'too much whisky rubber ankle' feeling.

He may as well have put a musket to my temple and pulled the trigger. I'm going to be useless for hours now. The sensation of lips depressing mine, a silky tongue tracing over the slice in my lip over and over with the devotion of a man mapping a clit, his other hand now harnessing my head to his face, it's pulling me into a vortex of carnage.

Long hair tickles my cheek and half-inch eyelashes snag mine, his eyes so very close they're midnight narcotics sending me into psychedelic dimensions of subjugation.

I hate noses, they always get in the way.

His tongue slides over mine and my desire explodes with instant utopia. I'm drizzling with anticipation, my pulse thrumming a rock concert in my ears, and I'm sucking the exploration delving into my mouth, my breath shaky, everything that constitutes 'me' is shaky under the sensory onslaught and delirious heat generating spiritual friction between us.

Sipping on his tongue, wishing it was something else entirely, I close my eyes against his intrusive stare. Wilting against his torso I feel a little reckless. The calibre of his gaze when I reopen my eyes obliterates all responsibility and prior commitments. All bets are off.

This... I'd die for.

Be careful what you wish for.... whispers a pirouetting shadow, still dancing the raven's ballet.

Inquisitive fingertips trace my neck and he murmurs gruffly, "Who gave you these bruises?"

"M...aartin."

"I'm going to kill him," whispers in my ear, my hair crimped between fisting fingers in silent suggestion of dominion.

Warm lips claim my lower lip, sucking me into his mouth where he bites the cut so hard all I can taste is blood, the edge of the table etching a permanent mark into my back from pressure, and the world slips unsteadily off its rails.

Good thing he has the grip of a thief or I'd be rugging the floor right now.

Chapter 3

After pilfering my sanity with his potent kiss he releases me to lean over, picking up my form and holding it to the lit candle.

The flame elongates, licking the edge of aged paper with hungry ignition, curling a ribbon of curdled smoke into the air, incinerating the fragile kindling so that he's forced to drop it into the dish collecting powdery carbon.

"What are you doing?" I demand, ever so mildly panicked that this gesture implies expulsion from his elitist train.

What? Do I kiss like a guppy or something? Did I fail 'the test'?

Leaning on the edge of the table for support I wish my legs would solidify and hold me again. Dread is burning a lava trail through my solar plexus and it's making me breathless.

Glancing down at me with his deviant smile, he caresses a warm hand down my arm, "Do not fear Ni-koh-lette, this is how we do business here."

"Do business? By burning contracts or waivers or whatever? I don't know much about business but if I tried that at the bank they'd arrest me for tampering with evidence."

"Koh-lette... chérie, do not be so full of fear. Dare to trust a man knows what he's doing."

Framing my face in his worry thawing hands, I'm instantly harpooned and can't think in a linear fashion. Whatever we were saying no longer matters one iota.

Trust a man to know what he's doing... amen padre! This man is currently pulping my willpower with a primordial stare which is fishing in my eyes for my soul, his bodily imposition pressing indomitable power into my wobbly bits and forcing my overwrought aorta into erratic palpitations. Thank god he's wearing a jacket or my nipples would be shaming me in their attempt to stake his heart directly through his shirt.

Holy fucking bananas I'm a mess. This is primal, impossible to resist, delightful and forbidden.

And that makes me want it even more.

He called me Colette. That was kinda sexy. Kohl-ette, ooooer fuck me to Tuesday that's hot. Kohl is black right? It's like being called 'sweet little black shnookums', and it's adorable.

"Whaa… why'd ya burn it?" I manage to enunciate as if I secretly devoured his entire single malt collection inside the picosecond he deflected his attention.

"Hush woman, does it matter why?"

Not particularly, but… well that was just fucking strange and even though this is über romantic and making me hornier than a devil's thorn I need some logic to cling to as an anchor in this hurricane of sensation.

Obstinately quiet I try the eyebrow arch to extend my insistence for an answer, because the hands on my face have slid to support me on either side of my ribcage and his thumbs are so perilously close to my erect nipples that I'm about to squirm, or blush, or beg, or…. faint. When is a good time to inform a hottie you're ticklish and about to spasm? I've been known to knee tender bits when I lose control in tickle torture.

"It sets the deal forever. Burn it and it is done. Written beyond, before and after, we remake fate."

"How holistic," I manage to mumble, all breathy like one of those lame dames in a romance novel. Oh lord above I've turned into a stereotype. "Nothing makes sense."

"It will," he murmurs, lifting my arms up to trail kisses to each elbow, and now I'm screwed. Infusion directly via lip to bloodstream is making me molten flux.

I'm gelatinous and have the thought capacity of an amoeba.

All focus is centred on his lips and how they feel, leaving a wasteland of want in their wake, the forge burning in my body making me desperate enough to dry hump his leg. I'm so ready he could make me pop with his pinkie finger.

This is satanic it's so incredible. I don't care about rules and regulations, or propriety or expectations or monogamy... I want it... **now**.

Coaxed to move, I'm bodily lifted, the thud of a heel connecting solidly with a door vaguely registering while I wallow in the incredible scrub of stubble exfoliating my neck.

Sucking occludes reason when his lips clam around my earlobe, his face nuzzling in my hair, jagged breath scything into my ear around the soundtrack of a dead-bolt slamming into place.

A delectable tongue traces the arch of my throat in the eye of the stubble tornado and my head is instantly drowsy heavy, the world whirling around me as I hit wanton warp speed.

I'm overheating, anxious, needy, happy to be left to feebly kneel on the floor to cling to knees and bury my face in his crotch.

I don't care if I'm labelled the prostrate pariah, there's only one artefact in this room I want to know intimately.

Shadows fall and open, curtains shimmy aside, all to the meditative lull of wheels on a track.

Dumped in a cosy quilt of comfort and style I'm engulfed in the sedation of desire, on fabric so soft it can only be his bed.

Fighting to lift my head I lose the wrestle and opt for a provocative tilt, curling my arm under my head and forcing my hipbone to protrude as I pull my knee up for stability.

By the light of a single flame I watch the mystery disrobe. His jacket is already gone... somewhere... and I'm fascinated by the binds which hold his shirt closed. No buttons, just cords, so many cords, on the sleeves, the front, the breeches... it's shamanic magic binding a soul into subservience.

Or keeping it restrained.

I hope he restrains me.

Laughing softly I watch the unlaced shirt part, exposing ridges and vales that definitely put Martin into the past tense category.

Sitting next to me his shoulder length hair falls forward when he pulls his boots off, standing again in a gust of displaced air when the breeches are unravelled and peeled off.

Clarity gongs, lucid panic sets in, and I sit up, immediately clearheaded.

What the hell am I doing?

Anton says nothing, he just prowls over me so I'm forced to recline for airspace, his eyes so soot dark they shine like midnight mercury, and I'm enveloped in his unique aftershave, trilling my pulse into a staccato so shrill it's training for the opera.

My breath clots in my throat when he presses chenille warmth to my chest, covering me in the Anton skin-blanket, sedating me with a kiss so deep I'm cast into a dervish of vertigo.

Lost in the cashmere arms of destiny I close my eyes to ride the waves realigning my tectonic plates. Determined hands find purchase on La Perla and I feel exposed when air paints across my leaking sex.

Instantly vulnerable, I inhale tension.

Squeezing my eyes tightly I am afraid I'll lose my nerve if I open them. Curiosity is whipping me while terror knifes through my heart when those insistent hands press inside my thighs and widen me so much I have no dignity left to claim.

My silk negligee is scrunched under my hips, knees are staked inside my own, and ruthless hands hold my wrists.

The second his exhalation hits my sensitivity I squeak, harp tense, my eyes snapping open, and I try to sit up, to recoil.

Adrenaline surges, giving me strength, but all I can see is the dark canopy tenting the baroque bed and the caliginous outline of pale me effectively pinioned while he samples my lady bits.

Gasping, writhing, I'm immobilised when he lifts his head to bark, "Koh-lette, be still."

It's an order, issued in a tone which brooks no negotiation.

And as if he owns my very soul I'm left bereft of strength by his legion-strong command, sagging heavily into the luxurious prison of his bedchamber, stripped of free will.

Elbows strap my legs down when he moves, it's rather uncomfortable. His tongue slaloms into me and I'm so oversensitive that the pressure of his nose detonates my impending orgasm, yanking a throaty explosion of passion out of my mouth.

I love noses.

Swallowed in the catatonic vulcanisation of sexual release, I relax, 'trusting a man to know what he's doing'.

Dowsing, nibbling, plunging and plundering, he sucks on me as if this is his feast and he's a starving man. He pours gasoline on the fire and it's all I can do to breathe.

It feels like he's draining me; siphoning my spirit through Satan's sanitation system.

Bang... bang thump!

"Nicki! Colette! Please open the fucking door!"

The urgency raging to crash in vaguely coasts across the ceiling, but I'm in carnal gallows, riding to rapturous insanity, they who shout are inconsequential right now.

Somewhere Jim Morrison is laughing at them, knowing no one breaks through to the other side, it's invitation only fuckwits.

Guzzling gobbling sounds infiltrate their way through my psychic fog and I reach out to stroke his hair, crooning nonsense in decibels of appreciation.

It's impossibly scrumptious the way he manages to tickle covert niches no lover has ever reached... I'm reeling, spiralling through galaxies on endlessly tilted axis with every new claim on my uncharted landscape.

Adoration morphs to discomfort. Adulation amputates when my body convulses in what I can only compare to a period cramp.

God. What the hell was that?

"Anton," I gasp, just the mere act of speaking enough to cause another sharp spike of discomfort.

He lifts his hand, holding up his finger in that 'just one moment please, I'm busy here' gesture.

Yes, I know you're busy there, do you think I don't fucking know that? You're an all or nothing kinda guy, am I right or am I right.

He sucks so hard it feels like I'm aborting directly into his mouth, and I scream, my pores exploding in distressed sweat, the pleasure annihilated.

"Anton!" I plead, beyond caring now, hating the punishing grip on my wrists keeping me tethered supine to his bed.

Jesus!

My arteries are coagulating, I'm shivering with excruciating agony, and I feel like he just literally 'ate me out'. Not in a good way, at all. Shudders pulse across my bones the way they do when I first go into shock.

Tears dribble hotly into my ears and I'm reduced to snatching handfuls of his hair and yanking, not letting go in the toddler form of Chinese torture. Gripping for dear life, holding my hands in tight fists swipes the final vestiges of my energy.

Thud!

"Colette! *Please!* Don't do it! **Please Colette!**" Bang.

Shoulders are getting shiners as they pound relentlessly into the door in the adjoining room. The voices beyond are wailing in torturous suffering, becoming weak and faint.

Maybe it's just me? Maybe I'm on the precipice of passing out? Sensation is being obliterated by throbbing injury.

Anton lifts his face to look at me and his stubble is covered in globs of blood.

Oh god.

Eddies of delirium flirt with my senses, my shaking becoming violent, my stability capsizing as my stomach roils.

He reaches out hands to claim my breasts, purging tension into them with enough force to bruise, saying in a conversational tone, "I had to. They seeded inside you to multiply themselves. They used you as their personal incubator, planting their souls in your uterus to manifest bodies. They are a virus infesting your body and feeding on you. A phantom possibility has no right to you, has no right to invest their seeds to multiply into physical reality through your womb. They have no right to claim you. Only I do."

Moving his hands he pulls the taut skin stretching over my stomach, "This is mine. You, are mine."

Right. Sure. That makes perfect sense you fucking lunatic!

"Light, switch on the blasted light," I shriek, hurdling into hysteria with one easy skip.

His beastly shadow skims the darkness and more candles are added to the first until they are generating enough heat to concave corneas. It's like mass in here, does he do communion too?

Struggling onto my elbows, I peer down, my raw nerves eroding, severing in quakes of disbelief at the dark blood pooled around my hips, into my favourite negligee, into his bed. I spasm compulsively, wracked in shock waves of revulsion... of denial.

It's brutal bed baptism. I'm scarlet, his hands have smeared my blood all over me like brands of misfortune, creeds of corrupt devotion, runes of curse.

My vision blurs in a whirlpool of revolt and I flinch when his silhouette straddles me. A gentle hand cups my head and cradles me to his chest, strong arms lock me close and he rocks me. "Shhh chérie, I will always protect you, even from my own greed. It's in the contract."

Weak, afraid, I have no strength to fight. Disabled, mutilated, I cannot run. I know I should be aware *and* concerned that Martin knows I'm in here and knows what I am doing, but all I can manage is simpering squeaks, sobbing against the man who has ruined me.

I'm haemorrhaging.

I'm going to die.

We can rule out opposition to biting. It's lost its appeal for me now. Who blew out the candles?

It's very dark... very... v.e.r...y... d.....a......r........k

Chapter 4

It's so silent. Unnaturally quiet.

Dispelling slumber I rouse myself enough to sample the first sweet breath of morning.

A bold thumb rubs across my cupid's bow and a sultry voice trickles seductive syrup into my ear, "Good morning, chérie."

Uhmmmm.... oh yeah.

A lady could get used to hearing that before she opens her eyes in the morning. It's a pocket of comfort in a lover's haven. Rich and creamy and hellaciously sexy.

The second I open my eyes and see Martin with long hair and uncharacteristic stubble, I peg upright. Fright left to fester overnight comes on strong in revisitation while my joy ferments.

Arms that could rock climb in a typhoon plant either side of my hips and he leers over me as if he's caging a feral animal.

"Koh-lette, the day you look at me in fear is the day I cut out your eyes. Change your countenance."

Shrinking against pillows while my stomach makes infinity symbols, I stare at my hands, breaking eye contact, needing answers, needing to scream, needing to re-evaluate the playing field, fast.

"Mon chérie, I was never the monster, *they* were. But they are no more, I removed the lesions adhering to your motherhood, I captured the parasites."

I prudently decide to start conversation with the mundane. "Monsieur, why is it so quiet?"

"Monsieur? You insult me Koh-lette."

Stress bites through his fingers when their relaxed length curl into intimidating fists.

Images of Martin beating the shit out of me flash-frolic through my awareness the way images are played in a subliminal cinema.

Was that a dream?

A heavy sigh blows the hair off my face in his annoyance and I watch those fists like a paranoid schizophrenic seeing hallucinations. They move to rest inside his elbows when he folds his arms, outlining a crevasse in his chest which simply serves to compound my anxiety.

He's the grandaddy don of the look-alike contest. He's the prototype they aimed to replicate. But he has a palpable presence, living breathing domination and power, and it exudes from him even in silence.

Avoiding eye contact at all costs, I watch his hands.

"Okay, I can see you're feeling disagreeable this morning. I haven't sent for coffee, but propose a toast in its stead."

Nervous, I watch long legs clad in black move, sensing him leaning to a bedside table, listening to the clink of glass on glass, maintaining a locked gaze on the ruby divan.

I want to go home.

Where is Martin?

Why isn't he looking for me?

A martini cocktail glass is offered under my nose, breaking my fixated gaze.

It could be full of water, or vodka, or gin, but it's clear as the vessel holding it.

"To us. To renewal. To making mistakes and never being afraid to correct them. To our courage… to *your* courage. To your resilience, and mine."

Terrified to offend him lest he decide it's grounds to chop off hands, I accept the proffered chalice, sniffing the contents suspiciously.

"You are supposed to toast, Koh-lette," he reprimands, his tone dark enough to jar me out of resolution and engage his stare.

Swallowing thickly I chink the rim of my sceptre against his while an invisible force squeezes my chest to a pinpoint of pain.

His formidable eyes enforce an involuntary lift of the drink, forcing me to sip crystal fire. My eyes water, it burns all the way through me as effectively as acid, leaving me raw and scalded inside.

He won't stop until he's destroyed me from the inside out. Is this some kind of twisted game? Cremate the beating heart and enjoy the preserved husk so you have an effigy mummified with charring alcohol? One who is nothing more than a marionette for you to pierce with your strings, to play the loving pantomime when you... you... ate what makes me female! You took out of me what defines me as a woman and you expect me to sit here like a good child who doesn't react?

Anger gives me false courage and I demand, "Why is it so quiet, Anton?"

He makes me wait, taking a leisurely draw from his glass, glossing his lips and igniting a latent power in his eyes, "Because we are mostly alone. You are not stupid, Koh-lette. You have your papa's looks and his intelligence. I told you I have destroyed them, consumed them, or for want of a better term – I have assimilated them. Multiple fractures are now a single clear facet. And because of it we are now on skeleton staff."

He reaches out and claims my hand in his, reminding me who is imposing here and who is diminutive. "That is why it is so quiet."

Clearing my throat, wishing the fire from the liquid crystal would abate and stop burrowing through my stomach lining, I defy self-preservation by probing deeper, "Last night you mentioned a contract. You said you would protect me, even from you...it was in the contract. Anton, what contract?"

Giving me a level stare, he lifts his chin marginally as if squaring for confrontation, his lips betraying him by pursing to white, "The one you signed with my blood. The one I burnt in front of you so it could never be undone. I was delusional once. I thought you should be martyred for your sainthood. I thought I was invincible. Instead what I did was unleash a legion on one woman and lived to watch you suffer by my hand, over and over again while I was imprisoned in my own greed."

He waves his free hand around, indicating the room, "This train, it is bliss-blitz. It rides on ethereal power, fuelled by my mistakes and of them there are plenty, enough to keep us hell-bound for eternity. This Express embodies my avarice, my delusions of grandeur, it exposes my warped conceit and inflated ego. I thought I could have the best of everything, even if I procured it by ill gain."

Looking away, slamming his drink onto the table I have yet to see, he shouts bitterly, "I have confessed. What more do you want from me?"

"Let me go," I whisper... terrified of the consequences.

"And where will you go Koh-lette? Who will take care of you? You cannot leave this train, it is your destiny. You vowed you loved me, and I have loved you from the first moment I held you in my arms. You were so tiny, so perfect, so pure."

Pouncing up he stabs a finger at me from the edge of the bed, "I raised you! You swore you loved me and would never leave me! But you did, Koh-lette! You abandoned me for men who aren't half what I am. Weak and pathetic impostors masquerading as your true love, yet you let them hurt you, suckle you, you gave birth to them and then laid with them the way I did with you! You destroyed me! I suffered! I cried, I self-flagellated, I mourned, I screamed, I begged, and it never ended until I used the one thing I have that they don't. My brain! Intelligence to outwit the whole lot of them even though they would have you believe I was dead and decomposed! In your heart you must have known why you loved them! Because you wanted *me*!"

I'm only now aware that tears are coursing down my cheeks and my head is shaking side to side.

He slides aggressively back across the bed, seizing my hand and holding it to his rough cheek, "You swore it. I love you papa. I'll never leave you papa. I'll never be like mama and leave you. You have *me* papa, I'll take care of you." He flings my hand back with such forceful thrust I smack myself in the cheek, "Do not make promises you can't keep because they bind your soul as surely as calcified rock! You locked us together forever by promising. But when I swore an oath to love and take care of you, I meant it Koh-lette. It nearly killed me but I made sure a part of me was out in the world, holding your hand, keeping you fed and warm, and kissing your nipples until they went harder than my betrayed heart."

Covering my ears, I need to flee. He's nuts! Last night was hot, and sexy, until it became seriously fucked up, and now he's telling me this is some kind of soul contract, a vendetta, a promise... involving incest! My own and his. No fucking way!

Flicking the divan away from my legs I examine my body, the bed, all of it blood free and perfect.

This place clearly induces madness. I would swear on the bible what happened was real, yet it clearly was a nightmare. He's accusing me of dreams where I featured but which we never incurred.

Worming, I place my liquid fire on a black table with a silver knob on the drawer.

Slipping off my side of the bed, I announce, "I'm going back to my room now."

"I never treated you as a child! When you became a woman you got the respect and adoration due you! Don't crucify me for loving the woman more than the child!" yells after my retreating form.

I force myself not to run. Count Anton is obviously a stage name and he's one amazing character actor. He came seriously close to getting me to believe his bullshit story. His script is so carefully versed to peddle exoneration for Oedipal sacraments.

I am going to behead Martin if this was a hoax he instigated.

Very funny Martin, I hope you aren't too attached to your balls because I think you owe me a new set of earrings for putting me through this.

One for each ear... or nipple... it all depends on how forgiving I am coerced into feeling.

Maybe it was a test of fidelity. Well I failed. It won't be the first thing I fail, or the last. I'm not perfect, and if you don't like that well sod off.

Chapter 5

Padding barefoot down the thickly carpeted passage I pass many closed doors on my way to the suite.

Annoyed, I yank the curtains open as I traverse, exposing reinforced panes of glass. Outside are endless cliffs of burnt ferrous rock.

Striations of cardamom and Dijon-mustard battle with ash white on the sheer walls, and I assume the railroad tracks run the length of some abandoned river bed in a desert.

There are no deserts in the UK, so where the hell are we?

It looks like Sedona from this limited perspective.

Pausing to crane my neck, I stare up the bulleting steep walls blurring past the window. It's as red out there as it is in here. We could be on Mars for all I know.

Whatever.

Huffing, glancing anxiously behind me to make sure I'm not being followed with a tranquilliser dart, I find my room and twist the handle, relieved when it opens.

Diving inside I slam the door shut behind me, whispering loudly, "Martin?"

I check the bathroom, the bed, and run instantly out of options. Pausing long enough to don the complimentary robe, I run back out, sprinting down the car, into the dining coffin, through that coach and into the lounge, charging with my heart racing to the observation carriage.

It's empty.

Not a soul.

Not a sound but the wind whistling a haunted requiem through marginally open windows.

This isn't possible. They're messing with me! Come on you jammy bastids, jump out and yell surprise now.

Please?

Deflated, I swivel, traipsing the long way back, determination solidifying my marrow.

Walking purposefully past my assigned suite, I try every door handle, each opening without so much as a squeak, unveiling five empty rooms that look like they haven't been occupied in a decade.

Worry begins the weevil gnaw through my calm.

This isn't happening.

Moving deeper into the Personnel Only section I find toilets as sterile as a hospital, tiled to the ceiling, a storeroom, a laundrette, the vacant kitchen, until I have nowhere left to go but four doors.

One leads to the locomotive, one to *his* quarters, leaving two unknowns.

With a trembling hand I twist the handle on the closest door, flinging it wide, knowing in one glance it's a bedroom, probably belonging to Tweedledee and Tweedledum.

Leaving the door open I try the last door, banging it wide, discovering the haystack of blanched bones. It looks like an archaeological dig, and the smell is fetid.

Gagging, muffling my nose with a firmly clamped arm, I step in deeper, seeing the hatch to the furnace.

Oh god! It wasn't my overactive imagination, it's real!

Squealing like I stepped in roadkill, queasiness giving my insides the Heimlich, I run willy-nilly all the way back to the kitchen.

Staring at long stainless steel tables, state of the art 'modern' fridges, I fling open the walk in fridge which every caterer owns.

Puddings are setting in perfect porcelain, marinades are hiding all manner of machete mangled morsels, and I dare to investigate deeper, moving through the plastic strips to the freezer.

Butchered carcasses hang on hooks, swinging a macabre dance with the motion of travel, and with the rime mummifying them in ice it's impossible to identify body parts, or animal type, because the cocoon is as effective as a plastic bag suctioned over a corpse in asphyxiation. Forget the Twilight Zone, this is the Snuff Sarcophagi reserved for Cardinal Kilt.

Hinging back, my toes freezing, I run to the exit, blasting through the closing door with all my might.

My pulse is galloping, my insides under attack from terror seizures, my eyes so wide I fear I may never blink again, falling onto the floor in the semicircle defined by three pairs of feet.

Who's running the train? Who's driving?

There has to be someone else here who can help me.

Molly smiles at me, shaking her head, "What are we going to do with you?"

Scrambling to my knees, backing up defensively while I boost out of the squat, I'm flush up against the fridge door with Anton, Molly, and Hyena-face.

I'm panting desperately, as if I'm running out of oxygen, my body temperature soaring. Panicked, I look at my only ally. He might be mad but he's my only friend in the sanatorium.

He smiles, offering me his elbow, "Need an escort?"

Where to?

Out of options, I nod, needing to know where they put Martin. Play the game, Nicki. Play the fucking game or the queen loses her head.

Anton smirks at the mismatched Siamese twins, "Coffee, in the lounge I think."

And as if I'm wearing my ballgown, he guides me out of the kitchen and into the corridor, walking his bitch to the 'lounge'.

Chapter 6

It's a Mexican stand-off while we stare each other down from opposite chairs.

He's dressed, still in character, insinuating I time travelled to this train of debauchery and corruption. I'm beginning to feel like the only sane person in the asylum. It's a great way to keep prisoners on board. To leap from a car travelling this fast would mean certain death, at least terminal maiming, and you can't leave.

Sipping his coffee, he looks out at the crimson walls hemming us in, guiding us as surely as a river down a gully. "What you fail to comprehend is we have a contract. Your signature, my blood, a fatal bond to both of us. We are sworn and locked together forever. Never to part, never to die, and never again will I share you, it is written and you agreed. No one but me, Count Anton Martin Dubois, has the right to your body, your soul, your love."

"Yup, sure thing," I nod, humouring his unhinged psyche.

Baleful black eyes snap their focus on me, "You don't believe me?"

"Is that a trick question?"

"Don't you remember Diurinish? When we stood at the burn and vowed our eternities together? We swore it in music, in blood, with sacrifice on the altar which became our bed."

The edges of my vision are smudging, my periphery dancing with the wild bucking of devils at full moon.

They celebrate.

What are they celebrating, exactly?

Woozy, I put my coffee down on the quarter table conveniently placed next to each couch.

"Where's Martin?" I ask, my voice coming out garbled as if we are fathoms underwater.

"You want Martin? But I told you I was going to kill him. Did you doubt my sincerity mon chérie? If you want him, he's inside me. Speak, he will hear you regardless."

"Help me…. please," I whisper into the den of opium-fogged lunacy.

I feel like my soul is coming undone, the world marbling and melting in demonic swirls of warped reality as if I'm channelling Dali.

How do I get off this train?

"We start again, Ni-kohl-ette. I have removed the ancestors we sired, our karma is expunged, now it's just you and me, we have a new lease."

His face lingers above mine... smiling... am I slumped? Did I swoon?

Desperate to sit up, I can't, vaguely focussing on wide leather straps.

"… for your own safety of course. You were hysterical darling."

"No! Martin! Help me!" I wail hysterically.

"Shhh chérie, I'm right here. Let me kiss it better."

My vision is blacking out in wild gyrations, the room a mishmash of textures and colour while it heaves in the high seas of my dissolving logic.

Saliva snails down my neck, air blowing cold across my breast when my robe moves...

… tickles and sweetness...

… caresses and kisses...

… the wet heat of an orgasm...

… sweat dripping off the ceiling onto my forehead...

… the relief when the crushing weight lifts off me and my lungs can expand without hindrance...

"We start again, this time our son will be pure and strong, part you, part me."

He'll want to abduct you to his den and have lots of babies with you.

Blinking against the bright light in my eye, I catch a glimpse of Anton's smiling face, his mouth blood red and drooling sanguine sin.

He leers over me in a distorted shadow, whispering softly in my ear while carelessly pinching my nipple for his sadistic amusement, "Blood of my blood, flesh of my flesh, in this worship we do not sin. We are holy Koh-lette. This is how it was in the beginning. Zeus did it. Enki did it. Nebro did it. Yaldabaoth did it. Saklas did it. By whatever name you wish to call the creator of mankind, he did it. The entire generation of Seth came about the same way, a father takes his daughter's innocence and enslaves her, and she is a good subservient wife who obeys his commands for all eternity. If we are to be gods my darling, then we must surely do it too. I create you, I mate with you, immortality is ours. Simple. The difference in our unity is I love you, I respect you, I leave you with a modicum of power. I promised you we'd begin again, and I will keep you safe, here....................

................with me."

Everything warps to galactic nothingness.

Chapter 7

Pegging up in bed, I look at the bright white walls and the door which is so very far away.

In a chamber with nothing in it but me and this bed I weakly squirm off the cot until my bare feet are planted on the floor, keeping my eyes riveted to the black window in the top half of the white door.

It swings open and a man in a white coat fills the entrance, a clipboard in his hand, a whistle around his neck, a pen-torch in his pocket peeking out shyly.

He smiles at me as if we are old friends.

"Martin?" I whisper, disbelief mingling with relief.

"I see you are up and about. How are you feeling this morning?"

"What? You'd know the answer to that better than me! What kind of stunt are you pulling?"

He's closed the distance, standing in front of me looking bemused, and so adorable I'm tempted to cut the tough chick act and fling my arms around his neck to weep, knowing I am rescued, I can escape.

Lifting my hand he moves warm fingers to my wrist, "Your pulse is good this morning."

"What? Stop fucking with me! I'm tired of the mind games!"

He gives me the angry look reserved by his twisted sire, Anton. "Colette, we've been through this already. You are projecting delusions onto me, and for that matter the other staff too. Whatever sin I am guilty of it's all in your mind. I promise."

Suddenly memories ambush me. The way Martin examined me after he attacked me in ghost form. The timepiece I picked was a nurse's watch. I even once thought the very words *paranoid schizophrenic*. Them banging on the door – was I hurting myself? Were they trying to gain entrance to save me?

Open the fucking door. Colette! Please! Don't do it! **Please Colette!**

The light in my eyes this morning.... his torch? Checking pupil dilation?

The buckle under my hip, was on my bed?

Anton holding me down so I couldn't move... was that from retraining straps because I was having some kind of... mental... episode?

Oh god.

I'm fucking crazy.

I'm one psycho sonofabitch.

I'm mental!

And my name is Colette, clearly.

He gives me another compassionate smile, guiding me to sit on the gurney, "Molly, up her meds for a few days. She's separating from reality again."

Snapping my focus to the door when he says that, I see Manic Molly standing there in a perfectly fitted white zip up uniform with my watch pinned to her pinafore.

What is it with that woman and uniforms?

Why do memories overlap? Do I have schizophrenia?

"What about the train?" I whisper, confusion trickling despair out of my eyes in spiritual condensation.

He lifts the whistle, "We use it when a patient attacks. That's your train whistle. The piper is your therapy. We've found you are easily pacified if we play that music to you."

Molly walks away to get my 'meds', and the only thing that bothers me is the clicking of high heels. I thought nurses had to wear noiseless shoes?

His eyes narrow, his smile eerie, "There's no escape. You didn't really think I'd let you go that easily?" A possessive hand traces knuckles over my cheekbone, licking a callus at my eyelashes, "You are the church where I worship, the altar where I pray, you are my religion. The body is the temple. We could rule the world, Colette. I will consume you, lay with you, for eternity, you are what keeps me alive. Our cast-offs never end while we procreate... until we have the perfect child. The saviour. You are blood of my blood, flesh of my flesh, and what we perpetrate is holy communion."

Slapping his hand away I flee to the window, desperate to know what's truth and what's not.

The world is normal beyond the windowpane. Meadows roll away in spring's glory, the sky cobalt and serene.

I'm in the nut-house. I...I... *the prison is my own mind*.

Turning back, shrinking into the cold rigidity of the wall, I feel caged and helpless when Molly walks in with two tumblers, tiny plastic cups so I can't break anything or stab anyone.

He nods, as if knowing my inner monologue, "You do, self-mutilate that is. You've been trying to cut me out of you, apparently. I can't say I'm not flattered that you think I'm so very powerful that I can own your fertility."

Did I just imagine our conversation? He's acting like a normal shrink again. My therapist. The-rapist.

My legs feel like jelly and I cling to the mesh covering the window, sliding when my feet lose grip, just catching sight of the smiling man in his kilt as he strolls past the window with dragon bones cresting his shoulder.

He gives me a conspiratorial wink, lifting a finger to his lips as if we have a grave secret together.

What?

What the wonk was that?

The room jerks, a machine chugs, and even Molly lurches toward Anton / Martin for a split second.

Awareness dawns when the landscape starts moving, catching speed and loping away fast enough to blur.

"It's a mobile psychiatric ward," she splutters.

Unconvincing, even to a loon like me. There goes your Bafta, bitch.

I recognise the kilted Captain when he fills the empty doorway, making it three to one in here. "Top of the morning, hen. Did you like my wee tune? Did it make your soul sing?"

I shake my head, unnerved, bewildered.

He shrugs, as if he couldn't be arsed either way, moving his attention to Martin, "Shall I start breakfast then?"

Anton nods, I know it's him because I just spotted how cleverly he hid his hair. It's a wig!

"Who are we having?" asks McMorain.

My blood desiccates...

I have to get off this accursed train. I have to!

Anton holds up his hand, in that 'one moment' gesture, stalking to me with the meds. "Take them, Koh-lette."

What choice do I have?

I'm outnumbered, I have to play along.

I swallow them, the room immediately disintegrating into milky apparitions. Skeletons walk around to flirt with shadows.

Skeleton staff.

He shines that light in my eyes, checking my pupils. "Just count back slowly. Everything will be fine. I promise I'll take care of you, chérie."

A locomotive screams sweet sacrifice and triumph, the bones incinerating, the souls separating, expressing scalding steam to kiss the white lightning striking across the beautiful clear day, churning billows into the clouds which are lowering a curtain of darkness on my hope.

C....ount.... back, slowly.

C...ount Anton.

I'm delusional.

Right?

The End

Author Biography

Poppet started her journey into fiction by telling horror stories to her friends before any of them hit puberty, and is still remembered fondly by her cousin for scaring the pants off all of them as little children.

Describing herself as more tenacious than the herpes virus or a virulent strain of syphilis, it would appear that no amount of antivenin, antibiotics, Armageddon, doomsday end of the world prophecies, or rejection letters from publishers, can dissuade this woman from writing.

She has spent a large portion of her years since she could 'walk again' (she wasn't born again, don't worry, put the smoke cannister down, it's safe to answer the door), writing paranormal romance and romance horror, taking the odd detour down fairytale lane and diabolical alley (which was a cul-de-sac ending with two floating eggs in formaldehyde).

She has over forty novels to her credit, ranging from the theologically challenging to botany for beginners; is signed to three publishers, and likes to self publish too. Her greatest shame is the first time she was published in New York it was for her poetry. It's hard to be a cool cat with that dogging her reputation. Perhaps her greatest achievement is counting wall tiles every time she uses a new bathroom.